THE STORIES OF

OF

GEORGE

ONSTOT

VOLUME 1

This is for Lynda Przybyla, who wrote me my first fan note. Wish I still had it.

CONTENTS

Also by George Onstot

BULLIES ON JUICE

TEE & A

RAGIN' CAJUN

BUM LOVE

WHAT'S YOUR PROBLEM?

ENTREPRENEUR

NATIVE GRRL

HOLE IN ONE

OH! BALLS!

A SUNDOWN WEDDING

On a clear, breezy morning in June, Jordan Hunt and her husband, Gabe MacDougall, sped east on the TransCanada Highway towards the small town of Sundown, where Neva, Jordan's oldest and truest friend, was to be married in her uncle's country house. Jordan kept the window rolled partway down and felt comforted by the cool air. In a few hours, she knew it would be a hot day. Gabe drove with both hands on the wheel. He had taken off his suit coat and hung it behind him, then rolled up his shirtsleeves. He had worn that suit, the best one he'd ever owned, to his own wedding several years earlier. A foot away from him, Jordan sat in moderate discomfort. She disliked fancy dresses almost as much as she loathed makeup and jewelry, and her shaggy hair and tattered clothing often amused her friends. Jordan could have spent her entire life wearing the old, faded clothing she had owned for years, but one could not go to a wedding looking like a Sally Ann poster girl. So Neva had taken Jordan downtown to one of their city's most exclusive boutiques, and Jordan had selected the peach-colored dress she now wore on the morning of the big day. She felt afraid to squirm, sweat or fart, and it occurred to her that simply sitting in the car might wrinkle the seat of her dress. She felt now the way she had some years earlier, when, as a small child, she had been dressed up and driven to her little friends' birthday parties. She took off her shoes and reclined her seat a little bit, spreading her legs in the most unladylike fashion.

Gabe wore a suit five days per week but disliked dressing up even more than Jordan did. A downtown litigation lawyer, he owned a dozen dark suits and three dozen sober ties. He also had plenty of hiking and fishing gear. He had shown Jordan the joys of the great outdoors, a world she had learned about on TV and in books but seldom experienced firsthand. Her parents were city people who, if anything, feared the wilderness; Jordan had scarcely smelled the woods or touched trees until she started hanging out with Gabe. Together they had gone on countless walks through every nook and cranny in Pioneer Park, studying and photographing everything that moved or made a sound. Then they did much the same on the islands that dotted the Georgia Strait. When finishing season arrived, Jordan sat nearby as Gabe stood waist-high in the water and the two talked for hours. Jordan, Gabe and Neva had all grown up together in Vancouver. Jordan, the daughter of an American father and Canadian mother, had spent the first dozen years of her life in Dallas. When her mother decided to return to Canada, she sponsored her husband and daughter. The three Hunts went to the immigration office for an interview. They signed long pink forms and flew up to the Great White North. They moved into a modest house and Jordan observed that it rained for the first thirty-two days of her life in Canada. Half a block away lived Gabe, fourteen, and she remembered herself as a sloppy, garrulous twelve-year-old checking him out on the rugby field, a muddied, bloodied man-boy *desperate* to win. Looking at him now, she could see the boy he still very much was, and she acknowledged to herself that she had loved him all this time, and always would.

They had all attended the University of British Columbia, but Jordan and Gabe had not resumed their friendship until she was getting a master's degree in art history and he had become a hustling young associate at an old law firm. They were married several months later. Neither of them could understand why people got married despite scarcely knowing each other; to have a successful marriage, they both believed, you had to have known that person all your life.

Jordan knew the way to Neva's uncle's house as well as she knew her own address. She had stayed there many times as an adolescent and visited frequently as an adult. Gabe had proposed to her on one of their long walks around the property. Jordan remembered that day so well because Gabe, asking her to marry him, had to speak above the din of the chirping, cawing, screaming wildlife surrounding them.

They turned off the highway and onto the country road that eventually led to their destination. The sun still had to rise some, and Jordan could see dew on the ground and leaves. She rolled down her window all the way and inhaled the lovely freshness of nature, of newly cut grass and chamomile. She closed her eyes and smiled. To be in a car with your husband, traveling to the wedding of your best friend, who was getting married at a grand old house you knew so well...what could be better than that? The only thing she was ashamed of, and felt badly about, was the fact that her husband had not been the first man to see her in her new dress.

Jordan had recently broken up with her lover. To say this to herself—*I had a lover, I cheated on my husband*—would have made her tsk and feel contempt if she'd heard someone else say it. The other man, David Jameson, was an older, immaculately groomed man from New Jersey who had moved to Vancouver to exploit the Canadian minerals market. Like Jordan, he fancied himself a writer—he had written this and that, been published here and there. They had met at a cocktail party hosted by *Canadian Life* magazine. His wife, Rikia, had recently taken a job with an exclusive public relations firm. His children were grown and had moved away to chase their own dreams. He amused himself by investing in dot-com startups, and was taking his time in writing a book about the relationship between economics and geography.

A few months before her wedding, Neva had taken Jordan shopping on Robson Street for that dress. The two women had visited every narrow, ostentatious boutique and department store in that part of town. In and out they went, Jordan wearing a very presentable suit which, in a dozen changing rooms, she shed with the indifference of a beach girl stripping down to her bikini. Each time, Jordan looked at Neva as if asking, *Is this one OK?* and the saleswoman stared in wide-eyed admiration, as if to ask the tall, voluptuous woman with the twangy Southern accent, *Have you any idea how beautiful you are?* She eventually settled on the peach dress...or perhaps simply let Neva make the decision for her. She took it home in a fancy box. Back in her living room, she put the box aside, peeled off her suit, unhooked her brassiere and put on the clothing she liked best: A horribly faded Judas Priest T-shirt and ancient Levi's. Then the doorbell rang, and David Jameson stood before her as rain came down in torrents. He gave her breasts the tiniest pinch, his usual greeting. "There's my glamour girl."

He tried to take her into her arms for one of their prolonged tonguing sessions, but she said, "Come in and have a cup of tea. I've just been out shopping for a dress."

David laughed, looking at the box. "Looks like you've been to the fanciest joint in town. Let me see the dress."

Jordan opened the box, pulled out the dress and shook it out. "See?"

"I want to see it *with you in it*. You are so beautiful, you have such a magnificent body…and yet you dress like a slob."

"Asshole." She draped the dress over the back of her seat. She went over to a sofa and sat. He joined her.

"This has to end," Jordan told David.

"What has to end?"

"*This.*"

"A wedding happens and you decide we have to call it quits? Is that what you are telling me?"

"No. *I'm* married, *you're* married and the preacher-man back in Tex-ass said that adultery was a sin. *That's* why we need to end this thing."

"That's an awful thing to say."

"Sometimes the truth is an awful thing to hear."

He snarled at her. "Sometimes I'd love to punch you right in that perfect little nose." He took her hand in his and they sat in silence for a while.

David hated silence, so he spoke up. He took back his hand and patted her on the thigh. "Maybe you're right. A little time apart might help us."

She shook her head. "Wrong. No more month-long separations. We're *over*. You go back home to your missus and I'll just keep on keepin' on with my hubby as if you and I had never happened." She swallowed hard.

David sighed. "I guess this couldn't go on forever."

The rain came down even harder. David and Jordan sat together for the longest time, holding hands. At some point he got up and left her sitting there. They did not see each other again.

Several kilometers down the blacktop was a dirt road that led all the way to their destination in Sundown. This far into the valley, they were surrounded by mountains and trees and the big city had become a memory. Gabe drove slowly because the road was downhill.

"Look ahead!" He pointed at a bald eagle as it

hovered just above them before soaring away. "See it?"

"Yeah! Wonder what it's doing this far out!" Jordan had always loved those majestic birds. She had watched on TV how the eagles in Louisiana and Florida swooped down and made meals of the wretched swamp rats that ate up the coastal vegetation.

"Let's get out and stretch," Gabe said. Jordan nodded and they climbed out of the car. They stood together, and he smelled of pine and fresh air. He went to put his arms around her. "Not too tight," she said. "Remember my dress."

"This is a big deal," he said. "Not like *our* wedding."

Jordan smirked. "As I recall, we didn't exactly *have* a wedding."

Gabe nodded. "Exactly."

They had gotten married at Vancouver City Hall, at noon, and after lunch at a fancy restaurant, he had gone right back to work, because his firm had many cases of expensive litigation that required his immediate attention. "I enjoyed our lunch that day," he said, pulling her body next to his.

"I really don't care if this dress gets wrinkled," Jordan said, throwing her arms around her husband. They stood in the front of the car and made out like teenagers.

Breaking up with David had been the mature, sensible thing to do. An affair could be compared to a hole that needed to be repaired. Old Mr. Wil Cross' property had had several such holes, and he had mended them so well that one could not tell where those holes had been. Standing on a dirt road kissing her husband, having the car serviced, sending emails, preparing meals, making arrangements and doing errands…such things could mend the spot where an affair had been, and repair it so well that Jordan had an easy time pretending that her affair had never really happened at all.

Mr. Cross had ordered the caterers to erect a large tent on his property, right next to his small house. When Gabe and Jordan pulled up to the expanse of grass that had been designated as a parking lot, they saw Mrs. Blandford directing servers on where to place tulips on tables.

"Jordan! Gabe! How delightful to see you!" she said, giving Jordan's hand a firm squeeze. "Your services are needed. Gabe, go say hello to Duncan. This is the bride's day, and everyone's ignoring the poor groom. And Jordan, you need to go see Neva upstairs. She's having wedding-day jitters and needs a friend right now. Tell her she needs to eat."

Upstairs, Neva sat on the bed in her wedding gown, taking hits off a joint and staring into space. Neva, round, pale and down to earth, wore her black hair pulled back in a ponytail. She and Jordan had been chummy since Jordan's family had moved onto Neva's block. Each summer, Jordan and Neva moved to this house in Sundown. In this bedroom they had smoked pot, drunk beer, fantasized about their futures and, once, tried making out with each other. Both girls declared themselves totally heterosexual (although Jordan could hear Neva's moans and felt the girl's hands on Jordan's lovely young American breasts).

"Is my old man still there?" Neva asked over her shoulder as Jordan entered the room.

"Yep." Jordan sat next to Neva.

"Does he still want to marry me?"

Jordan shrugged. "Far as I know."

"This sucks. We would have been better off to go to city hall, like you did."

"Well, you didn't. Anyway, your uncle says this will be his last wedding, so you better make it a good one."

Neva inhaled and blew out a long stream of sweet smoke. She passed the joint over to Jordan. "Marriage marks the end of my childhood. I was having *such* a good time. Why am I getting married?"

"A marriage is a good thing for a woman," Jordan said, taking a hit.

"Look who's talking," Neva said with a smirk.

Jordan giggled. "Oh, that. I broke it off with David."

Neva's mouth opened wide. "No shit?"

Jordan shook her head, smiling. "Nope."

"When did you call it quits?"

"The day you and I went to buy this dress."

"*Why* did you dump him?"

Jordan thought for a moment. "Because I knew that I was doing the wrong thing. At the time it felt good, but afterwards I kind of hated myself. So I just said, 'David? Fuck off, goof.'"

"Ouch. Are you glad?"

"Sometimes. Other times I miss our afternoons

together."

"Poor baby. Maybe marriage is intended to make us miserable."

"That's a fine man you're marrying today."

"Then why am I so ambivalent about him right now?"

"Because you're stoned and famished. Your blood sugars are low. Your brain chemistry is out of whack."

The windows were open and the smell of cannabis mingled with myriad other farm odors.

"Were you unhappy on your wedding day?" Neva asked.

Jordan puckered her lips. "It didn't mean that much to me. We got married because his family and mine said, 'If you're going to spend the rest of your lives together, you need to get married.' So we said, 'O.K.'. No big deal to me. Not like yours."

"I wasn't at your wedding."

"You didn't miss anything. It was over in five minutes."

"I felt badly about that, Jordan. I wanted to be there for you."

"You had a good excuse. You were writing an exam."

Neva shook her head. "No, you don't understand. I really wanted to be there and see how uncomfortable you were, standing there with Gabe, exchanging vows that you didn't particularly believe in." She squirmed a bit. "Shit, man, this dress is so uncomfortable. Now I know why you like dressing down."

"Well, I was sent up here to bring you something to eat, so what do you want?"

"Just bring me something yummy."

Jordan smiled. "Done."

She came back with a platter of toast, bacon and coffee. Neva munched away and said, "Give me an update. It sounds very busy down there."

"Gabe and Duncan are having a guy-talk. Everyone else is taking turns kissing your uncle's ass."

Neva chuckled. "Surprise." Then, "I'm so hungry, I could eat lots more of this. Be a dear and get me another helping."

"No can do. After your vows, you can pig out. They've got an entire table full of mints and cashews and shit. Don't eat it. You'll barf."

Neva drank some coffee and said, "I feel like I have so much pressure on me right now. I'm glad this thing will be over in a few hours."

"It will be over in thirty years," replied Jordan.

"Ever heard of something called 'divorce'? And did you *really* dump David?"

"I sure hope I did." Jordan took another toke and said, "During those two years, it seemed like one Jordan was humping David on the sofa while the other Jordan was Gabe's dutiful wife. In many ways it was a boring affair. You had better flings than I did. I envied you. David was the closest I'd come to an interesting affair. I thought that after breaking up with him the two Jordans would become one again, but that hasn't happened. Sometimes I have to step in and prevent the two Jordans from beating the shit out of each other."

"Give it time," Neva said. "You'll get over it."

"Actually, I don't think I will," Jordan said.

After the bride and groom traded vows, everyone sat down to lunch. Servers carried trays of champagne; plates were heaped with food, devoured, heaped with more food, gobbled up again and taken away. Neva and Duncan cut the wedding cake to loud cheers, and Jordan felt grateful that the bride and groom didn't mash the cake into each other's face, something she had witnessed at recent weddings. Throughout the meal, the happy couple went from table to table, saying hi and thanking everyone for coming.

Jordan and Gabe were meant to sit apart, for reasons unknown to Jordan, but they sat together anyway. Neva's mum surely noticed that they had switched place cards and shot them a puzzled look, but Jordan and Gabe smiled and winked at her, so she said nothing about it. During the ceremony, Jordan had nearly wept at the beauty of it all. At lunch, she and Gabe held hands under the table and played kneesies. Jordan sighed and beamed, as if she had gone on a mysterious, frightening trip and returned to find her world intact and delighted to have her back.

When the servers began pouring coffee, Neva left her seat and hurried over to Jordan. "Baby let's cruise," she whispered.

Holding hands, they hustled over to Neva's Miata convertible and climbed in.

"Shit, man, my dress is all wrinkled now." Jordan chuckled.

"Fuckin' shame." Neva fired up the Miata's

engine. She headed to the road that encircled Sundown's big, beautiful Lake McMahon. "I brought some weed," she said, holding out a couple of joints.

They stopped at a point directly across from the tent. Separating the girls from the house and wedding guests was the lake, and after turning off the car's engine Neva and Jordan took turns staring at Lake McMahon's clear glassy surface.

"I wonder if they think we've eloped," said Neva.

Jordan shook her head. "They know where we are. They can see the car."

"Maybe they think it's rude of me to take off like this."

"No, they probably think you've stolen a few minutes to hang out with me." Jordan lit the joint, sucked on it and passed it to Neva.

"Goodbye, childhood. Hello, adulthood." Neva groaned.

"In case you haven't noticed, we've been adults for

quite a while now."

They smoked some more and stared at the lake, then looked across the distance and gazed at the house, tent and wedding guests. Jordan felt fairly sure she could spot Gabe and Duncan talking to Neva's uncle, who owned the million-dollar property. When the time came, Neva would inherit the whole shebang, but that day was probably a decade away. She looked more closely at Gabe and felt her heart pound. *If you only knew...*

The trees blocked the sunlight, leaving the topless car dark and cool, just the way Jordan liked it. She could picture David at will, clothed or naked, here or there, talking or silent. Some things, and people, stayed in your head long after you wished them to disappear. She could picture him sitting there, waving to her from across the lake, not two dozen steps from the man he had cuckolded.

Neva crushed out the joint. "Guess we better head back. We've been away long enough." She turned to Jordan. "Doesn't life just totally weird you out sometimes?"

"Life is what it is. Life isn't weird. People are weird."

"I feel as if I'm living a dream, but not always a good one. I try to take a step forward but I'm afraid I'll fall through the cracks."

"Deal with it."

Neva revved up the Miata's engine and got back onto the road leading to the dirt parking lot, the wind whipping through their pretty wedding clothes. They drove back to the people who loved them and the wonderful lives that awaited them.

EATING OUT

"That's what I love about you," said Liam. "You're thirty-five and yet you have this thing about you that makes me feel like a pedophile. Even with your big fat butt."

"Whatever," said Bonnie. "But in this relationship, *you're* the jailbait."

"No way! No way!" Liam giggled.

Bonnie laughed in spite of herself. In truth, she had nearly a decade on him.

The two sat at an outdoor table at a fancy restaurant in downtown Vancouver. They felt mellowed out from the ubiquitous plants and gentle ocean breeze. The mountains hulking in the background, too, somehow made them feel protected, although Bonnie could not have said from what or whom. It was all too gorgeous, and she felt very grateful to be a part of such beauty. Liam leaned over towards her, breathing through his nose, and for an instant Bonnie thought he looked like a dog sniffing another's ass.

"You're thinking things right now," Liam said.

"Yes."

"Talk to me."

"Well, I was just thinking about how much effort had gone into this restaurant, making it this fancy and special, and how the manager is probably standing back there, putting his foot up his workers' asses to make sure we like eating here and come back for more. All of this so that, when the check comes, we pay up. It just seems so phony and hypocritical."

"It's here for us to enjoy. We come here, they treat us well and feed us plenty, we pay up and go away. We choose to make the experience good or bad."

"Oh, I think you know what I'm getting at. The whole thing about a 'date' is so fake, too. We're on our best behavior, as opposed to being our natural selves, and we come here to be fed and pampered." She sighed.

"Damn, I'm out with Miz Party Pooper. Can't we just leave our worries and problems alone while we're here? I can assure you they'll still be there when we leave this restaurant." A couple of years earlier, after a handful of spectacularly bad carnal relationships,

Bonnie decided that sex was good for populating the planet, spreading diseases and not much else. So she resolved never to screw anyone else. ("Becoming a professional virgin might turn out to be the best decision I've ever made.") She let Liam hang around her because he young and handsome, because he was already seeing someone else, and because she liked the way he stared at her breasts.

Liam worked as a freelance journalist and Bonnie ran an alternative high school. Both people had very few, if any, true friends, but they had many acquaintances, and one such person introduced them to each other. He had contacted her regularly for a couple of years, inviting her to travel functions or calling just to make forgettable conversation. Over time they went from occasional coffee dates to actual meals at her apartment. Liam had long since dumped his girlfriend, so Bonnie said OK when he said, "Let's get on the sofa and snuggle." Liam, nearly twice her size and far less inebriated, soon pinned her, and she exclaimed, "Uncle! Uncle!" His feistiness at first aroused her, then confused her and finally distressed her. He forced her legs apart and hiked up her dress, licking his lips at the sight of her white panties. For a moment she felt nineteen again, being groped or masturbated by some boy in his pickup truck, which was not altogether a bad feeling. Still, she yelled at Liam to release her, and after a few more minutes of slapping and snarling, he did just that.

"Liam," she said, pulling her dress down past her crotch, "when you said you wanted to snuggle, I thought that was *all* you wanted. You're clearly quite an attractive guy, and I enjoy spending time with you. But I do *not* want to have sex with you. I'm much too messed up in the head for that, and I don't want sex to get in the way of a good friendship."

Liam nodded. "Messed up in the head. That's my Bonnie."

"Yeah, well, some very nice people are messed up in the head."

"The same hole that has opened up so many times before will open up again."

"Fuck you, Liam."

He smiled. "Exactly." His voice was full of levity, but she still perceived him as a potential rapist and her wine buzz disappeared. She made a fist and said, "Liam, I don't want to punch you out, so don't provoke me."

He sat back, that predatory glint gone from his eyes, and made a glum face. He left soon thereafter, giving her left breast a pinch on the way out.

She went to sleep that night thinking he was a prick and she was better off alone, but the next morning she kept thinking about his big body and hungry eyes. She called him and invited him over for dinner. They got it on in the bedroom, on the sofa and in a half-dozen other locations. Several weeks later, they sat in the fancy restaurant, feeling very smug.

"I wanted to go in there and take the thing very seriously," Liam was telling her. "The man has some serious creds, right? I think he's helped many people. But then he tries to put the make on those women half his age. That's his real hustle."

Liam had been writing an article on spiritual well-being and the renunciation of materialism. He had just attended a weekend workshop led by a guru from the Sixties, and the experience left him feeling very cynical.

"Well, maybe that's just his way," said Bonnie. "He likes young women. Many older men do. Myself, I see nothing wrong in that."

"I was, like, 'Bring it on. I'm prepared for everything.' But his kirtan performance went on for so long that I nearly fell asleep. Then he gave his talk and he was slicker than a greased pig. He was sort of saying, 'I promise you enlightenment in one weekend.' People said, 'How will I know if I become enlightened?' and he said, 'You'll know.' Then someone said, 'What if I know I didn't become enlightened?' and he said, 'Then I'll know you *did*.'"

He shook his head. "I mean, what the fuck?"

Bonnie paid some attention to what he told her, and appreciated his candor, but what really interested her was the curl of his lips when he spoke, and the fineness of his hands when he gesticulated. Whenever he came by to visit her, he would make some sort of face as he knocked on her door so that, when she peered at him through the peephole, she would see him smiling, scowling, glowering or making some sort of ugly, contorted expression.

"Liam," she asked, "how come you make those faces at my door?"

He threw back his head and roared. "Isn't it great that I can do that? Our relationship is based on honesty, right? So sometimes when I come to get you, I'm feeling happy, or sad, or angry, and I let that emotion show on my face when I'm at your door because I know you think that's OK." He leaned forward, eyes closed, and she did the same, letting her lips rub for a delicious moment against his.

"Plus, I love the look on *your* face. When you open the door, you look so girlish and frightened. I think it gets our evening off to the right start."

Bonnie rolled her eyes and said, "Well, Liam, I think that's all very weird but touching. As the cliché goes, 'I don't believe I've ever met anyone quite like you.'"

"Sweetie," Liam said, "don't take this the wrong way, but I'm probably the first decent guy you've dated. The rest have been total fucking goofs."

The two had agreed that Liam had been the best thing to enter Bonnie's life in a very long time. While she valued him and enjoyed entertaining him with tales of her bad dates with buffoon boyfriends, she felt at times that they were both laughing at her a little too hard. Liam seemed genuinely sorry for when she told such stories, he also appeared entirely too eager to hear them again and again. Just the other day, she had repeated her story of Vinny and the evening when they sat in his car and he leaned over to rub noses with her. He then said, "If a woman allows me to do that to her, she will go to bed with me. Rubbing noses is simply a way of asking for sex."

Liam buried his face in his hands, the way he had done at an Ellen Degeneres performance when her jokes made his laugh till his sides ached.

"What a good-looking, pompous dickhead!" Liam had cried out. "I can't believe he would say such a thing. Why did you let him degrade you like that?"

"Hey! I kind of liked it. It was like I was a teenager and going out on a date with Marilyn Manson. We'd dress up in Goth, with black lipstick, and freak everyone out."

"Marilyn Manson! Goth! Freaking people out!" Then, "That guy who rubbed noses with you? Did you let him get into your pants?"

"Liam—"

"Sorry. Sometimes I forget to use my brain before I open my mouth. So what became of you and Vinny?"

Bonnie told him a few more Vinny anecdotes, but stopped after she became convinced that Liam had started laughing at *her* rather than at her misadventures. "I'll never be able to rub noses with anyone ever again," he said.

A server brought them appetizers and wine. They told him they needed a minute, so he went away.

If Bonnie's old boyfriends were guys Liam had never met and had to imagine for himself with Bonnie's help, others were men Liam knew, or knew of, well. Perhaps the best of the worst was Bryan, a paunchy cross-dresser who also happened to be Liam's favorite radio personality. Liam knew that Bryan broadcast from his home studio, and pictured the deep-voiced radio star sitting at the control board, his flaccid pectorals and potbelly tied up inside a corset as he read colorful news items to countless listeners who knew nothing of the patina of rouge on his cheeks or the fruity perfume on his hairy neck. Liam could no longer listen to him without cracking up.

Liam, too, had had girlfriends, but compared to Bonnie's losers after his imagination had caricaturized them, Liam's girls just basically chewed gum and hung out. He usually said little about them before shrugging them away, but once in a while one or another of them would come to life, and Bonnie would learn more about that chick than she cared to know.

"The last time I had a relationship like this was with someone named Candace," he'd told her as they lay naked in each other's arms. "It was kinky like this—she was kinky like you—and what made it special was that we didn't acknowledge the kink. We treated all the freaky shit like normal stuff. We fucked hard and long and I talked dirty to her because that seemed like the thing to do. I told her things like I was a pedophile and she was my prey, and I could just see her face color with repulsion. Afterwards she seemed really disgusted, as if I'd humiliated her with my bad talk." He shrugged. "It was just role-playing and fantasy. I don't know what her hang-up was."

Their server arrived with salads, soup, more appetizers and steaks. The sun had descended and the sky had darkened into an azure that made Bonnie beam. She knew, just then, two things in her life: that she had fallen in love with Liam, and she would break up with him soon. She would miss him for a while, but he would find someone else and forget about her. Her thoughts of Liam, and feelings for him, raced and wrestled inside her head. She paid them no mind and tried really hard to listen to what he was saying.

"A part of that weekend was a workshop in which they wanted us to talk about our sexual fantasies," Liam told her.

"Did they really get into the down-and-dirty stuff?"

"No, it was just the usual nonsense, like this guy who's been wanting for the past thirty years to bone Bo Derek, and he finally gets his chance and she's frigid. Or some other guy wants to pork his wife while they're skydiving."

"Maybe they felt uncomfortable so they withheld their raunchier fantasies."

"Well, shame on them if they did," Liam said.

"Did they groove on *your* fantasies?"

"I didn't tell them mine," he said.

"Then shame on *you!*"

"After hearing their lame crap, was I going to tell them about my hot-and-nasty fantasies? I don't think so."

"If they were lame, so were you."

"I was not lame," Liam said, sitting up straight and squaring his shoulders.

"You were lame. You were just another guy in there, as embarrassed as the others."

"My hot fantasies were none of their concern. I was there in a purely professional capacity, doing research on an article."

She shrugged. "Whatever."

"There was one memorable moment. Some guy said that what really turned him on was the idea of making it with an Indian woman—Indian or Pakistani. Things got a little tense in the group, as if he'd said something that was totally unhip."

"Really? Interracial sex, gay marriage? You see that everywhere today. I'm surprised people would get uptight over something like a white man doing it with an Indian woman."

"Maybe I should have told them about when I screwed our Indian housekeeper."

Bonnie shook her head. "It's better that you didn't.

Nobody would have believed you."

"And yet it's true. I was, what? Sixteen, seventeen?"

The server brought them more food and poured them more wine. Bonnie, already buzzed, stuffed more scrumptious food into her mouth, not caring that it would go straight to her hips and ass.

"Tell me about your thing with the Indian housekeeper," she said.

"It happened only once. We had been checking each other out since the day my mum hired her, and one day while we were alone I invited her into my room to listen to some bhangra music. She was, like, 'OK, but just for a moment.' We listened to music and smoked some weed and I started feeling her up. She was just a year older than I was and she was beautiful enough to be in Bollywood movies."

"Did she speak English? What did you two talk about?"

"Yeah, her English was good, and she had a few hundred other family remembers back in New Delhi who wanted to move here, too. We talked about the usual things you talk about when you know the talk is really just foreplay."

"Did it turn you on that this chick you were going

to lay was the housekeeper?"

He shook his head. "Not really. I was just a kid and all I thought about was that I had this thing in my pocket and I wanted to stuff it inside this sexy Indian woman. But then my mum came home just after we were leaving my bedroom and she said, 'Oh, Liam,' with this sad shake of her head. To tell the truth, I *liked* it that my mum knew, because it sort of meant that I had confessed to diddling the housekeeper, so there was no guilt for me to feel. But whenever Inderjit and I saw each other around the house, and that naturally happened a lot, I would smile but she would look away, like, 'We have been naughty and that must never happen again.' I liked that, too."

They stayed quiet for a while and attacked their salads. Talking about sex and being naughty always stimulated Bonnie's appetite. She swallowed a mouthful of lettuce, bread and seafood, followed by a big sip of sweet, cold wine, then looked through the huge, immaculate window at the other diners. She noted their poor manners, how they cut their food with forks and chewed with their mouths open. She stared for a few minutes at the birdlike shoulders of an older woman in a pretty peach-colored jacket. The woman's body language screamed out about a lifetime of disillusionment, envy and stinginess. Suddenly, Bonnie seemed to sense that all the people in the restaurant yearned to have, through their ugly designer clothing, some sort of presence and participation in the world.

"You can't ignore racial differences even though we pretend that the differences aren't there or that they don't matter," she said. "A little while back my car was in the shop, so I had to take the bus. I had to wait, like, half an hour for the bus, and I was the only white person at the bus stop. I was wearing a very colorful outfit and felt *very* white and female and different."

Liam nodded. "Were you scared?"

"No, just really self-conscious. There must have been half a dozen Chinese and Indian teenagers at that bus stop, and I know how they like to make fun of people just to entertain each other. I felt I was a pretty easy target."

"My last time in Toronto," Liam said, "I had a weird experience kind of like that. I was running for the subway and its door closed in my face, so I made a face and pounded on the door. Then I saw these two black guys inside the car mocking my face and pretending to pound on the door. They looked at me to see my reaction, so I flipped them off. The bigger guy scowls at me and grabs his junk, like, 'You dissin' me, whitey? How'd you like to suck my big cock?' So I grabbed *my* junk and pointed at him. I guess to him all of that was hugely disrespectful, because he started

44

coming over towards me, and the damned doors suddenly opened!"

"Oh! Did he beat your ass up?"

"No, because the doors closed just then. But they were still talking trash at me as the train departed, and I kept flipping them off."

Bonnie laughed. "That sounds like you got some revenge. Wish I could do that—you know, grab my crotch, like, 'Hey, asshole, eat my cunt!'"

Liam shook his head. "You would be sending out precisely the wrong message."

"When I was I Europe, some street guy came up to me and started yelling at me in English, 'You cunt whore bitch, sucking on every man's cock.' His breath was awful, too."

"You have a knee and he has balls. Why didn't you put him out of commission?"

She shrugged. "I don't know why. it just didn't occur to me. But I like the idea of grabbing my crotch or something obscene like that whenever someone starts up with me. I like the idea of yelling back at that crazy guy, and we could have just kept it up, yelling foul things at one another."

Liam smiled. "I think it's adorable that you would consider doing those things. Of course, you would never do such a thing. You would go home and punch a pillow or have a nice big cry to get it out of your system."

Bonnie frowned. "Liam, why would you say such a thing?"

"What do you mean?"

"My adorable thoughts, punching out a pillow. I've never punched out a pillow. Also, I *have* yelled at people, many times, after they yelled at me. So stop it with the 'cute' and 'adorable' and 'little,' O.K.?"

"But you are those things," he said. "Take it as a compliment."

She rolled her eyes. "I have nearly a decade of life experience on you. I left home when I was sixteen. For the longest time, I supported myself by taking crappy jobs until I got on with the school board. You've never had a bad job. Your mum wiped your ass till just a couple of years ago, so what do you know about anything?"

His forehead furrowed; he pursed his lips for a moment. "I'm aware that you've had many experiences and you've had more than your share of struggles to overcome. But the thing is, your struggles haven't made a cynical, hateful bitch of you. You still have a fun, girlish way about you, and I really admire that."

46

Bonnie smiled and took a big drink of water. All she could say was, "Well, it's nice to be appreciated."

"Well, you should be appreciated," Liam said. "And I don't know why you've dated so many men who failed to do that."

They both stopped talking and resumed shoveling food into their mouths. Bonnie smiled despite herself, thinking about how long she had waited for her boyfriends to express such appreciation, and here he was, big handsome Liam, saying the thing she had always wanted to hear. It was a shame she would cut him loose soon.

The sky grew dark and the coastal wind kicked up. Soon, Liam and Bonnie were the only diners left on the patio. She finished her chocolate mousse, drank down her second cup of coffee and wished she had more of both. Liam started talking again.

"I'm concerned about that article I'm working on. I need to treat it seriously even though I know how ludicrous it is. Even the older, more mature ones were a joke."

"That's too bad," said Bonnie. "It would have been good if there had been some big man you could have adopted as sort of a father figure for the weekend."

Liam nodded. "Yeah, it *was* too bad. Unfortunately, the only guy there who could have filled that position was one of the team leaders, and he was, like, 'I'm bisexual and I'm OK with that,' and I was, like, 'Well, *I* don't swing that way, so hands off.' Also, the main guy there, who was this spiritual leader from the Sixties? He was, like, 'I'm as virile as a porn star and I get all kinds of pussy,' and he's saying this to a bunch of sorry middle-aged men who think they've lost all their sex appeal."

"But didn't you say those guys were married? I would assume they were getting laid by their wives."

"Didn't matter. Those guys all spoke up about how insecure they felt around women, even their wives, and they figured that as they got older, those problems would just get worse. All the while, Baba the guru, who's running the show, is going on about what a cocksman he still is."

"What did you tell the group? Did you admit to anything?"

Liam nodded. "I told them about my feelings for you."

Bonnie blushed. Liam had touched her. He could do that often. If he loved himself, and he certainly appeared to do just that, he could also love her almost as much. If he discovered something about her that seemed less than lovable, he valued it for just that reason—it was proof of her authenticity and humanness. "It makes you more real," he would say. In her presence, he had brought smiles to the faces of strangers—grumpy people doing thankless jobs—and at those times Bonnie told herself that she loved him.

"I had a girlfriend named Whitney," he had told her. "She was a mess, totally screwed up. I got her straightened out. I talked her into going to journalism school."

Their server came by to offer them more wine.

They said yes. Bonnie took a long drink and no longer felt chilled by the ocean breeze. "I was wondering," she said to Liam.

"Talk to me," he said.

"That time you did it with the housekeeper? Did it make you feel odd afterwards, when you constantly ran into each other?"

"No, she was OK with it. I saw her somewhere with some Indian guy downtown. He was probably her boyfriend."

He scraped at the last bits of his dessert.

Bonnie arched her eyebrows and waved her hand at him. "Hello…?"

He looked up at her. "Yes?"

"Tell me more."

"About what?"

"Inderjit and you. When you saw her downtown."

He smiled. "We said hello."

"Must've been awkward."

"Not at all. She was going her way and I was going mine."

"Liam," Bonnie said with a frown, "was Inderjit in Canada legally?"

Liam swallowed. "Why?"

"Just answer the question."

"Well," he said, scraping some more at his dessert plate, "I have a feeling she didn't, because my mum helped her get landed immigrant status, and Inderjit quit the day after that. My mum was angry about it. I'm totally uncomfortable with this subject."

"Why are you uncomfortable with it?"

"Gimme a fuckin' break," Liam muttered.

"You see," Bonnie told him, "when a girl is attracted to you, they want to date you, whatever 'date' means to them—even something as simple as small talk over coffee. That didn't apply to you, because you were the son of her boss, so she was sort of at your mercy."

He shook his head. "Absolutely, positively not. I did *not* sexually exploit our hired help. There was none of this 'I'll have your ass fired if you don't put out for me' thing. I would have tried to make it with her even if she had been our neighbor's pretty daughter."

"But would she have said yes if you hadn't been a member of the family she worked for?"

"I suppose." He puckered his lips and added, "But I do seem to remember that she reached for the door."

"She tried to escape?"

"Not exactly. It was more like, 'Condom! We need condom!'"

"Liam! Did you rape the housekeeper?"

He straightened up again. "No I did not. Are you trying to start a fight with me or something?"

"Oh, I could talk to you about your attitude about

those men at that workshop you told me about. Those middle-aged guys you thought were so comical. Did you stop to think that they worked like hell to support their families? That maybe they're doing the best they can to get by in this hard, cold world?"

Liam looked this way and that, snarling.

"Inderjit didn't want to have sex with you. That's why she tried to run away, screaming, 'Condom!'"

"As soon as I told her I'd withdraw before I shot my load, she said cool."

Bonnie imagined an Indian beauty putting her clothes back on after being mauled by Liam. The beauty just shrugged at Bonnie and said, "Shit happens."

"I did not rape anyone," Liam declared. "I don't have to do such things. I can get all the pussy I want just by asking for it."

Their server sneaked up to them. Bonnie asked him for the check. Liam asked for a Cutty Sark over ice.

"I should go now," said Bonnie through gritted teeth.

"Not yet." Liam reached over and squeezed her hand. "Let's get back to the happy place we were in a few minutes ago." Then, "She probably didn't want to have sex with me, or she was ambivalent about it. But that made her fairly typical of many women I've done it with. You also need to know that when I was younger I mistreated women all the time. I wanted only one thing from them. I let the little head do all the thinking."

"But Inderjit was different. She wasn't just another girlfriend. She was hired help, and you didn't treat her as a peer. The message you were sending to her, whether you knew it or not, were, 'I want to fuck you. If you say no, I'll get my mum to fire you.'"

Liam shook his head. "Bonnie, it wasn't like that."

"Then how come she was trying to get away?"

"Because she thought my mum might come home, catch us in the act and have her sent back to New

Delhi."

Their server brought him the Scotch over ice, which Liam accepted with a nod. He sat on the edge of his seat, with one leg crossed over the other, and he sipped the Cutty in silence, to show his displeasure with Bonnie. For the zillionth time, she admired his handsome face, his big body and the way he held himself. She shivered as a blast of costal breeze blew through her clothes.

"I wish I'd never brought it up," Liam said, taking a sip of iced Cutty.

"You're such a spoiled-rotten brat," she said.

"And *you're* a big-assed cunt."

They looked away from each other. Bonnie's legs started cramping up. She stretched them, felt no improvement and stretched them some more. She now considered their dinner a failure, and wondered if he would be offended if she insisted on, or at least offered to, pay half the check, which she knew would be a big one. She also wondered if she had enough cash to do so if he accepted her offer.

"Let me put it this way," she said. "You have fantasies about sodomizing receptionists and molesting thirteen-year-old girls. You like making believe I'm one of those girls even though I'm much older than you."

"Ho hum."

"Just wait. Your fantasies are a little weird, but so are mine, and I'm OK with that. But I have to think you were on a huge power trip with Inderjit. You took one look at her and thought, 'She's beautiful, she works for us, therefore she works for *me*. So she's mine for the taking.' Sometimes you seem to have a difficult time telling the difference between fantasy and reality. Remember when I told you that I had worked as a car wash attendant? You said, 'Why would you do something like that?' Like you just couldn't wrap your brain around the idea that people had to take bad jobs so they could pay rent and put food on the table. God knows *you've* never had to degrade yourself that way."

"I was trying to pay you a compliment because I didn't think you should have to do work that was so far beneath you."

She nodded, and they sat in the darkness for the longest time. She could no longer see his face, but could see the outline of his head and the breadth of his shoulders. He had a long, muscular torso, too. She could tension and indignation in his silhouette, the way he kept one hand on his glass of Scotch and the on his lap, his head tilted with insolence. He had not yet forgiven her for some of what she had said, and she knew he felt entitled to some sort of apology. Liam had a strength and pride she admired, and she predicted that as he aged and matured and grew, he would become the most enviable of men. She also knew it was too bad that she would no longer be in his world when that happened.

"You and I," he was saying now, "have a complicated relationship. I let you feel my sharp edges and I show you my dark corners. With Inderjit, it was *not* complicated. What happened, happened. If we didn't talk about it later, it was because we had nothing to say."

Bonnie again pictured Inderjit pulling on her underpants as she sat on Liam's big bed. Bonnie reached out to touch the housekeeper in empathy, but the young Indian woman slapped away the hand. She got off the bed, ran a hand across her bum to smooth out her panties and marched out with as much dignity as the situation would allow. Liam pranced along behind her, his eyes glued to her rump, and in the hallway they encountered Liam's mum, who shot her son a reproving look before going about her daily business. End of misadventure.

"It's weird and funny," said Bonnie. "You come back from that male workshop thing and get into this argument with your girlfriend about raping Inderjit."

"Yeah, and it wasn't even a rape." Liam guffawed and Bonnie felt better. She reached over and took his hand. They gave each other little squeezes and palm rubs.

"So," she said, "what did you learn from that workshop?"

"Mostly I learned," he replied, "that I'm damn lucky to be me. Not that I didn't already know that."

Bonnie smiled. "Too right."

"You should have see the others. They were, like, reviewing every moment of their entire lives, asking, 'At what point did I get so fucked up?' Although I don't sound like it, I really empathized with them. I'm really just glad that I am the way I am."

She threw back her head and laughed. She quite adored him, enjoyed every moment of his company and knew she would miss him after their breakup. She took a deep breath and loved the feel of the cold air in her lungs.

"Come on, big dude, let's get out of here before I freeze to death."

Inside, the restaurant charmed Bonnie with its warmth and beauty. Nearly all of the other diners had left, and she looked around the big empty space, feeling that she had it all to herself. A natty older couple sat at a corner table, lost in conversation. A few handsome waiters cleared tables with actorish elegance. She pictured Inderjit in Liam's bedroom, one hand with a decent purchase on the doorknob, then Liam, leering and drooling, pulling the housekeeper back to him. A few hours later, she rode home on a diesel bus as it rumbled through torrents of Vancouver rain. She shook a handful of Smarties out of a box and let the candies melt in her mouth as she crossed her legs, her vagina still sore from Liam's long, thick erection. An excruciating cramp tore through her left leg, and she yelped as she reached down and grabbed it.

"Sweetie!" Liam cried out, bending down and putting an arm around her.

The old people in the corner smiled at Liam as he snatched up Bonnie as if she were an inflatable doll. She wrapped her arms around his neck and looked over his shoulder as he carried her away, and she took a last look at the restaurant, thinking that she had never seen anything quite so beautiful.

ROBSON STREET

Someone once wrote that if you can see how you once loved someone, you still have deep feelings for that person. Well, recently, I, Jimmy Fairweather, a Vancouver architect, went to my office one morning and worked hard at looking busy. Then I put my computer to sleep and walked down to the Robson Street Starbucks to meet up with my pal Stan Ng and his new bride, Heather Rasmussen. Stan and Heather were still in that 'We're married! Can you believe this shit?' period of wonder that follows a wedding. They giggled like two people who had just survived a motorcycle crash, their bike mangled and shattered into a hundred pieces but they themselves remained miraculously unhurt. I tried not to be cynical and wished the best for then, but I had also been lonely and unhappy for a long time and their giddiness was starting to piss me off. Stan had brought along a bunch of pictures of their wedding, and as I flipped through them, I looked up for a moment and saw Katrina running by in her leotard, looking like a cover girl for *Anorexia Today*.

Even when we were together I had considered her way too skinny, although I reminded myself that way too skinny was better than way too fat. I also came to believe that I liked bony shoulders and backs, plus gaunt faces, tiny breasts and boyish butts. Forever dieting, she could always find a trace of fat on her body she needed to burn off immediately. She ran for miles or did a hellish aerobics session every day. I saw her now, racing along the sidewalk with a sweaty, flushed face as if she were running from something (maybe herself). She had a headful of permed hair—I hated perms—and people we had known commented that she was the kind of women who caused traffic accidents. Sure enough, as she ran by, pedestrians *did* turn their heads in her direction and smack into each other.

"Jimmy, isn't that Katrina?" Stan asked. He was the only one of my friends who, after my nasty court battle with her, had failed to respect my desire never to speak of Katrina again. He often asked about her, his head tilted and lips pursed, as if anticipating some fascinating scientific information. Naturally, I resented his inquiries and knew that, while Katrina and I were together, I had been stingy, nasty, dishonest and hypocritical towards her. I was big enough to admit that I had been a little asshole, and as I saw her come down the street, I told myself it was O.K.: I did not love her anymore, for what was love but a myth to inspire poets and madmen?

"Ooh, this is gonna be awkward," said Heather as soon as she figured out who Katrina was.

"No, it's fine," I told them. As she passed our outdoor table, I hollered, "Katrina!" Calling out her name, I felt immune to her considerable sexiness, so I did so again, this time in the casual voice of someone who doesn't care if his greeting goes unheard: "Hey! Kat!"

She had an iPod Shuffle clipped to her collar, and she blew by us on a rant from Eminem or Niggers With Attitudes.

"Didn't she hear you?" Stan asked.

"Guess not," I said. "She had her music up much too loud."

Stan sneered. "You call that shit 'music'?"

"Maybe," I said, "she was just ignoring me."

"I think that's very rude," Heather said.

We were sitting there on a late-spring morning under a cloudless sky, the kind of day Vancouverites get infrequently and value inordinately. We made a point of staying outdoors. I had my back to the front window, so I picked up the stack of wedding photos and had another look at them.

"Jimmy!" Heather gave my shin a little kick. "Katrina's gone inside. She's waiting in line. What are you waiting for?"

I did not care to go in there and speak to Katrina, but Stan and Heather sat staring at me, expecting me to get up and go inside or at least tell them why I wouldn't do so. In our little part of the world, we all believed in being in therapy or being one's own therapist, and in saying to oneself, 'Man up, now! Don't be chickenshit!' Sitting there with my two friends, I knew how much they wanted to see the manned-up Jimmy Fairweather. If I had been alone, I would have drunk down the rest of my coffee and buggered off home to zone out on CNN and MTV for a few hours with a six-pack of Corona. I stood up and muttered, "I'll be back." I traipsed into the coffee shop.

Inside, I stood directly behind her and could hear "Fuck whitey!" or something buzzing through her earbuds. I tapped her on the shoulder and she turned around.

"Hey," I said.

She plucked out her earbuds and said, "Oh, Jimmy. What did you say?"

"I said, 'Hey.'"

She nodded. "Oh, O.K." Then she frowned, nodded again and stuck her earbuds back in.

I went back outside and slumped into my plastic chair.

"She looks terrific," I told Stan and Heather.

"Better than terrific," said Stan.

"Much too skinny," said Heather, who had thunder thighs and a bubble butt.

"Too damn gorgeous," said Stan.

"Fuck off," I said. I sat and mooned for a few

minutes about my last few days with Katrina, even though I had promised myself I would do no such thing. I thought of the weekend following the *Michelin Guide*'s odious review of our gourmet restaurant, Katrina's of English Bay. The critic had devastated us by mocking my work (I had designed the restaurant) and Katrina's cooking. She had expressed ambivalence about my decisions concerning the restaurant's design and I kept my yap shut about how another expensive seafood joint was the last thing Vancouverites needed or wanted. The two-page review crippled our already unstable relationship like a blast from an Uzi. Katrina went ballistic. She stayed away from home *and* the restaurant the following day; touchy little Pierre had to run the kitchen all by himself. Katrina worked out that the gym, did a high-impact aerobics class, got a massage and, finally, rode her bicycle all the way to Tsawwassen and back. When she finally came home, red-faced and murderously pissed off, she accused me of being the shittiest boyfriend in human history. I slipped out to drink a few pints and let her cool off. When I came home, close to midnight, I discovered that she had moved out and taken all of *my* property, most of which I cared little about. I guessed she would donate my clothing to the Salvation Army.

What really hurt, though, was that she had also made off with collection of Grateful Dead memorabilia. I had most of the Dead stuff I wanted: posters, postcards and ticket stubs from their 1960s performances at the Avalon Ballroom and Fillmore West auditorium. I had handbills and advertisements from Ken Kesey's Acid Tests from 1965 to 1967 in San Francisco and Los Angeles. The thing I valued most was a handwritten letter from Bill Graham to Jerry Garcia congratulating him and the Dead on all their success. Katrina gathered up the entire collection and sold it for chump change to Doug Haslett, a prominent local collector. He just stowed it away with his Elvis and Beatles shit. To get back at her, I drove out to our locker at West Coast Self-storage, withdrew all of Katrina's antique, immaculate Barbie Dolls, put the lot on eBay and sold the little girls for just under two thousand dollars. When Katrina confronted me about her missing dolls, I told her the truth and wrote her a check. She tore it up, threw it into my face and sued me.

"What's wrong, Jimmy?" Heather asked. She looked young enough to be Stan's daughter. "You look kind of sick."

I wiped my face and didn't pretend to feel well. "I think I have to be somewhere else right now."

"Gotta go?" Stan asked. "Too bad."

"Yeah. Too bad." I just sat there. Then I turned and looked through the glass doors at Katrina.

"Jimmy," Stan said, "stop looking at her if she makes you feel uncomfortable. You can watch all the people go by here on Robson Street, or we can take turns admiring my new bride." He winked at Heather.

I nodded at Stan, then immediately turned again in Katrina's direction. "I should go back in there and try again. I really should."

I eased myself out of my chair and, as casually as I could, walked past Stan and Heather and headed for the glass doors that were separating me from Katrina. I had always felt like a doofus whenever walking from here to there in public, and now I felt clumsy and unkempt, clueless as to what to do with my arms and how to swing my legs. I swore I smelled foul, or perhaps just imagined it. I knew I had neglected my body, had let my gut get flabby and titties pointed. I walked up to the glass doors and pulled one open. Katrina, next in line, stood gazing up at the menu, although I felt sure she would order her usual rocket fuel. I stole up behind her and this time placed my hand on her shoulder the way a TV talk-show host would touch his favorite guest. Katrina turned around, her lips pursed and forehead furrowed, and stared at her shoulder as if I'd just vomited on it.

"Me again," I said with false cheer as I removed my hand. "How goes it?"

"Fine," she murmured, stepping up to order. "Hi, Libbey," she said to the butch woman behind the counter, "I'd like a cappuccino."

"Still drinking that crap, eh?" I said.

"Still drinking hot chocky?" she retorted, eyeballing my paunch. "You're getting fat."

"Fat and happy," I said, sucking in my stomach. After cleaning out our apartment by giving away Katrina's stuff, I had no idea how much I weighed, nor did I especially care. I wasn't getting any younger, my hairline wasn't getting any fuller and I wasn't getting any skinnier. So who really gave a fuck? "You look skinnier than ever."

"Here you go," said Libbey, serving Katrina her cappuccino and offering me an empathic little smile, as if she knew something of my history with Katrina. Then I remembered that immediately after Katrina had taken off, I bumped into Libbey at some bar and we had a brief, beery, bitter talk about how it felt to be dumped by a woman, and she nodded with admiration and agreement when I told her that it felt as if you had come home to discover that your most prized personal possessions had been removed from your residence and now were in the custody of an asshole collectibles broker in North Vancouver.

"You owe me money!" I blurted at Katrina, meaning it as a joke. Alas, it came out as an accusation, even after I added a little nervous giggle at the end.

"Ouch!" Katrina said as she stepped around me and rolled her eyes. "Goodbye, Jimmy." She hustled towards the door as if being pursued by a gang of street toughs.

"Katrina!" I shouted, even though she was only a

dozen feet away.

She wheeled around and faced me, her eyes glittering with rage, her cup of cappuccino gripped in both hands like a can of pepper spray.

"I don't have to deal with you any longer, Jimmy," she said. "Barb tells me that I've already put up with enough of your shit." Barb, Katrina's therapist, had seen us both for a while. I alternately feared and loathed Barb—mostly feared her—so I quit attending our sessions.

"I apologize for my bad behavior," I told her. "I'll try to do better. I have a table out there with Stan and Heather. Let's sit for a while."

They were standing now and gathering up their things. I hurried out to them.

"Where the hell are you going?" I asked.

"Look," Stan replied, "if you two are getting back together, it will be World War Three, and we don't want to be around for that."

"Shush!" said Heather.

Stan patted me on the back. "Jimbo, you truly are a tortured soul, and you seek out other tortured souls so you can torture each other. You can't be happy

71

unless you're miserable. Enjoy your misery."

I laughed, called Stan an asshole and pecked Heather on the cheek.

"I love Jimmy. He's such a head case," I overheard Heather say as they departed and Katrina took Heather's seat. The air now felt tinged with an electricity that hadn't been there before, and the sky seemed more violet.

"So Stan and Heather finally got married," Katrina said as she watched them walk down the street. "She's got quite a bum on her."

"I think he likes 'em that way," I muttered.

"Whatever floats his boat," she said, shrugging.

We sat back and regarded each other with ambivalence, with much affection mixed in. We had parted with shouts, court dates, exasperated lawyers and legal documents. For us to be sitting there at a Starbucks table, smiling at each other over hot drinks, seemed as satisfyingly naughty as sneaking into a dyke bar together. Everyone—friends, parents, psychiatric social workers and police—had told us: *You are no good together. Stay away from each other or face the consequences.* Yet there we were, giddy as little kids hiding from the grownups. Many things had been absent from our relationship, but we had always turned each other on, and as I sat there and let my gaze slip down to her breasts, I felt my one-eyed serpent beginning to wake up.

"Long time, no see," Katrina said.

"You look terrific," I replied. "Love your perm."

"Thanks," she murmured, as if not quite hearing my compliment or doubting my sincerity. Or maybe she just didn't want to participate in pointless, polite small talk. She looked at me with the coldness of a surgeon perusing a patient, trying to determine where to make the first incision and how much blood she wanted to spill. She said, "I saw on iTunes that the Dead's entire catalog is available for download."

"Sure is," I said. "That's a very provocative thing for you to say."

She put down her cappuccino cup and I saw the outline of her arm muscles. I could smell her sweat, too, and remembered how much I loved her female odor in bed. "You ripped me off," she said. "You sold my Barbies for two thousand. They were worth so much more than that."

I let out a bitter, disgusted little laugh. "You started it. You stole my Dead stuff and sold it for, what, five hundred? Why didn't you just give it away?"

"You got two thousand and lied about it in court," she said.

"I got a decent price. Some of them were in poor condition."

"They were completely intact and totally beautiful. Prick!" She shook her head the way she did when observing life's most egregious outrages. She had called me a prick many times before, and that had been her nickname for my love muscle. But her levity was gone now. "You sold my little girls," she repeated, as if I'd made whores and crackheads of her daughters. I could see that she was reliving it all now, the vicious insults we had flung at each other, the fat scowling lawyers, the exasperated judge dismissing our suits and countersuits. I, too, began picturing our last meeting in the big empty space that had been Katrina's of English Bay, reduced to nothing but dangling wires, pebbles of plaster and a bare concrete floor. We treated each other with the most exaggerated politeness that day, perhaps because we were both tired of arguing and feared that our battle might become physical. I didn't believe in hitting women and, anyway, I knew damn well that she could take me in two minutes if it came down to a fight. "You sold their accessories and outfits, too."

"Well, I couldn't send them away naked. They'd catch cold."

Her eyes narrowed. "Don't get flippant with me!"

"Lighten up, Katrina."

"You sold my Barbies and *lied* about the money in court!"

"My lawyers told me to lie. They thought I could get away with it," I said.

She hooted. "Suem, Settel and Kashin! What a great choice of legal counsel, Jimmy!"

She got to her feet, and everyone at the other tables turned to watch her. I then remembered how much Katrina delighted in throwing public tantrums. *Here we go again*, said a voice inside my head. *Seems like old times.* I noticed the trembling of the hand holding her cappuccino cup, and hoped she wouldn't fling its contents into my face. At their restaurant, he had seen her throw beverages into employees' faces, had watched as she, empty-handed and enraged at someone over a trivial infraction, had picked through the dirty cups and glasses for liquids to splash on that person.

"Don't make fun of my lawyers," I said, even though I'd made fun of them, too.

I could see the telltale signs—darting eyes, twitching lips, the hand trembling even more; *Should I or shouldn't I?*—and then she did it. Fortunately, her cappuccino had cooled off a bit as its brown frothiness made a Rorschach stain upon my face.

I wiped my nose and nearly flipped her off, but then the people at the other tables started applauding Katrina and she squealed with delight at turning a bunch of strangers against me, and I felt my face burn with shame and anger. She stood up, curtsied to the people at the other tables, then half-danced off the patio of Starbucks and into the middle of Robson Street. I caught up with her, then grabbed and kissed her, overbrewed coffee dribbling down my chin, as traffic stopped and horns honked. A bus could have flattened us both just then and I would have happily soared into eternity with her.

BOBBIE DYER

Bobbie Dyer turned fifteen in the summer of 1975. She and her mother shared an apartment separated from a shopping mall by a major thoroughfare. The nearest crosswalk was too far away, so Bobbie jaywalked to the mall, which was the location of the Igloo, her favorite hangout. She brought her own skates, whites one that were neither the best nor the worst. Ice skating was her passion for the moment, and she loved its sensations—the constant coolness that was such a relief from the brutal summer heat; the smoothness of the ice, the gray interior that made the place look like an igloo (thus its name). She didn't show off like an Ice Capades queen, didn't try to outskate the others. She kept her hands at her sides and smiled as the cold air kissed her face. The music, disco tracks as mindless as rain, blared through the sound system. The boys, some of whom like pretending they were NHL goons, stayed away from her. They didn't spray her with ice or try to ram her into the boards. They didn't try to body-check her, make her fall on her ass. Maybe she sent them a message: Don't even try. I'm too fast for you. Or maybe they thought she just wasn't worth the trouble.

William Wellman skated at the Igloo. Lithe and fair, he had dirty blond hair and gray eyes. He smiled often, and sometimes without humor. William had negotiated the blind curve of puberty and sailed into adolescence with an aplomb that made him the envy of his peers. That year he had gone by "Wil," with one L. He had graduated from Claymore High School that June and been accepted at M.I.T. to major in engineering. Wil was the son of Mike Wellman, also an engineer. Wil's brother had attended Annapolis, his sister had gone to Julliard as a music major, and now the time had come for Wil to make everyone proud by being accepted at the world's most prestigious technical institute. After graduating, he would work at his father's firm, just as Shel Jameson and Stu Evans had passed the bar and joined their fathers' law firms. "That's how it is. Nice work if you can get it," said Bobbie's mother, Lynne. Bobbie nodded. Wil, she'd decided, was the most interesting thing around; he could have her friendship, if he wanted it. There were others who wanted him, too. She'd seen Ms. Laporte, their French teacher, staring at him, but the woman had somehow giggled and tsked at Bobbie, making Bobbie go pink with embarrassment.

Throughout that year, Wil had dated Steffi Moreno, and the rest of the school couldn't stop talking about them. Steffi, a tall, voluptuous, volatile Mediterranean beauty, threw kicks and punches when provoked. Her relationship with Wil astonished those who considered him conscious of social standing. She'd been orphaned, so far as anyone could tell—she drifted along, invulnerable to life's wallops; she stayed with this aunt or that older sibling, got a ride to school in a different vehicle every day. Her hair was the deepest brown, short and shiny as a mink's.

One evening, Bobbie watched Wil and Steffi at a Claymore High dance. In the darkened cafeteria with the music loud and the strobe lights flickering, she laughed to herself at the sight of so many dancing boys, as jerky and rhythmless as epileptics. Wil danced his own way, really not dancing, just standing there, eyes closed, hips slowly grinding. Steffi, too, moved little, hips grinding, not quite touching him but *almost*, playing chicken. Inevitably, of course, the vice-principal chaperoning the dance wedged himself between the two and pried them apart. Steffi squared her shoulders, ready to tell him off, but Wil, tickled by their nonsense, took her hand and pulled her away for some private time. They showed up together in the library the next day, ready to be teased.

Wil had plenty of acquaintances and admirers, Bobbie observed, but was too aloof to have what she would call "friends." He had easy access to a dozen cliques and moved in and out of them as soon as they bored him. Academically, he made top marks without much apparent effort. Bobbie had had one class with him—history—and thought his success was due to his retentive memory. (He'd had a bad case of something in his junior year and missed so many classes that he needed to go to summer school so he would graduate on time. Bobbie couldn't imagine handsome, bright Wil sitting in that classroom with all those remedial, sad-eyed misfits.) She knew that Wil read all the assigned textbooks within the first month of classes but he cared little about their contents ("They're written by and for idiots," she'd overheard him say). His reading tastes were mostly limited to monthly news magazines and nonfiction bestsellers with splashy covers. When their teacher, Mr. Manuel, called upon Wil, the boy smiled—he often seemed happy to have the attention. "Would you explain to us the three branches of government?" Mr. Braverman asked. Wil said he couldn't, but did Mr. Braverman know what Alvin Toffler had written in *Future Shock...*?

Steffi, after a dozen brief breakups, had dumped Wil and begun an affair with Roger Kettyls, who managed the Claymore *Times*. The newspaper, housed in a charming old brick building on a hill at the end of town, was one of Bobbie's favorite places. She loved to buy a Coke from the vending machine and sit in the small lobby, reading back issues of the *Times*. Kettyls had a master's degree from the celebrated

University of Missouri School of Journalism and, according to Steffi, felt a profound disappointment over ending up in puny, boring Claymore. He was a big, hairy, sweaty man, and Bobbie wondered how he felt about his great luck in hooking up with Steffi. (That was how she saw them—"hooking up"—his parts fitting into hers, then unfitting again, and probably separating forever before much longer.) He had a daughter, a dowdy, friendless girl, Beverly Ann Kettyls, at Claymore High. One day, Beverly Ann appeared at the Igloo while Bobbie was there. Beverly Ann traipsed around in her tattered sneakers for a few minutes as if looking for someone or something. Bobbie hurried off the ice and into the ladies' locker room. Steffi sat on one of the benches, massaging her feet, smoking a Kool and snickering as she smoothed out her leotard. Bobbie, standing off to the side, leaned against a wall and watched as Beverly Ann entered the room, lumbered up to Steffi from behind, grabbed a hank of Steffi's hair, pulled her head backwards and shattered her nose.

It happened so fast that Bobbie had to blink and tell herself that it was for real. Beverly thrust a chunky fist into Steffi's face, who fell with an "Oh!" as Bobbie caught her but later could not remember rescuing the girl. Someone screamed (Bobbie believed it might have been herself), people rushed in and carried Steffi away. Beverly slumped into a corner and waited for the police. An ambulance arrived; two big men in white shirts entered the lobby, put Steffi on a stretcher and drove off with her. The tinny music kept playing, but the skaters stopped and gawked at the cops, medical people and management. Bobbie looked around for Wil but couldn't find him. She knew he'd been there, that he'd watched as Steffi arrived. She put her street shoes back on and went out into the parking lot but his car, an orange Mustang, wasn't there.

Soon after the paramedics and police left, the managers closed the Igloo for the night, so Bobbie walked home. This was the year of mosquitoes. All the way back to her apartment complex, she had to swat away the insects, but they bit her anyway, even on the eyeballs.

STEFFI'S NOSE HADN'T been that big, but she insisted that her new one be smaller. "What's *your* problem?" she asked when people looked at her. It was as if she'd caught them staring at her breasts, which she was used to and didn't especially mind. She was taller and curvier than Bobbie; she had magnificent, jutting breasts, a heart-shaped butt, lovely long legs. She didn't have money for clothes so she went to the discount shops and bought whatever fit. Like many other beautiful women, she looked good even in the cheapest T-shirts and irregular jeans. Bobbie, of medium height and unremarkable looks, knew she would never overcome her envy of Steffi.

Beverly had been arrested, faced charges; Bobbie had to go to the police station to be interviewed. No trial happened—Bobbie kept waiting for one—and Roger Kettyls sold his newspaper, then moved away with his daughter. Wil Wellman, too, had taken off, and each time Bobbie passed his family's house on her way to school, she wondered how it felt to be Wil, to have a family with money and to know, since birth, that you could become whatever you wanted to be when you grew up.

Her own residence, a two-story apartment like so many others in her part of Claymore, seldom felt like home. Its architect, idiotically, had designed it so that its sole air conditioner sat in the living room; the two bedrooms, both upstairs, became sweatboxes during the relentless summer heat. So the two women spread out their sleeping bags on the living-room floor and tried to make a game of it—"camping out with all the conveniences of home"—as they slept a few feet away from the blasting air conditioner (they kept it on high because low was almost as bad as off and medium was broken). In the morning, they woke up shivering and sneezing. "This place is a joke," Lynne had said. "We're moving next month." But they stayed and stayed.

Lynne had kept some of her father's furniture, big heavy items like a sideboard, a gumwood mirror, the headboard of a bed. That headboard, nearly eight feet tall, seemed to have been scavenged from the seat of a Forties movie. Bobbie's grandfather, Lynne said, had been a doctor in Claymore. "You can't imagine how it was for him, Bobbie. People paid them as they could, or not at all. It was *expected* of him to provide treatment even if he ended up receiving no fee." Bobbie had seen pictures of him, a handsome man with serious eyes and a small smile, and convinced herself that she and her mother looked like him. The doctor also spent much of his career stoned on codeine. He died young and broke.

Naturally, Bobbie asked about her own father, a man she could scarcely remember. "How am I like him? Was he—" Her mother just shook her head and smiled. "He was just a guy I knew. You're here, I'm here and he's not. That's all that matters."

BOBBIE HAD SPENT her entire life believing that she had an inheritance waiting from an uncle in Canada—enough for college, a sports car, whatever she wanted. But when she came of age, she learned from her mother that the amount was lower, much lower. "I've had access to it," Lynne said when confronted. "This apartment isn't much, but it's not cheap, either."

"Well, too bad for me," Bobbie said, her voice laden with sarcasm. She and Lynne could annoy each other, but their conflicts and arguments were really just verbal slaps and cuffs, forgotten about moments later. Bobbie and Lynne mostly considered each other a best friend. The news about the depleted inheritance neither surprised nor disappointed Bobbie—somehow she had thought of it as a rainbow, beautiful but insubstantial. She knew, also, that Lynne was not ready to have her move out. Bobbie still thought of herself as someone who, like Wil Wellman, wasn't forever trapped in Claymore, someone who could escape into a gratifying, fulfilling life whenever she believed the time was right. She could stay and keep her mother company for the time being.

A few months after graduating, Bobbie started working at the Claymore Inn, an upscale hotel and banquet room near the freeway. People went there to eat prime rib or for special occasions like wedding receptions. The inn, a maze of large rooms and parquet floors, was kept dark and cool. At the inn, she became reacquainted with Steffi. Bobbie waited tables and Steffi was always stationed at the bar or card room. She was much as Bobbie remembered her, beautiful and distant, unafraid to talk back. She had gotten married, raised her hand so that Bobbie could see her chunky diamond ring. Their winter was endless and busy; each weekend, the Claymore Inn was chaotic with skiers; one tour bus arrived as soon as the one before it departed. Steffi acted as if she and Bobbie had run with the same Claymore High clique. They took their breaks together, laughed at and bitched about the same things and people as they sipped on bottles of Coors that were meant for paying customers. As often as not, Bobbie loitered for an hour so she could give Steffi a ride home.

Steffi's husband's name was Aaron Betts. Well into his twenties, with dark hair and a slight build, a constant smile and dimples. Bobbie decided he was just handsome enough for Steffi. "What does he do?" she asked. Steffi shrugged. "He's an entrepreneur," she said, being careful to say it right, even though Bobbie was fairly sure the girl didn't know what the word meant. Aaron dealt in moderate amounts of this and that, making sure it got from here to there. At first, Bobbie thought Aaron might be involved in stolen goods; later, she suspected he was pushing pot and coke. Sometimes things went wrong and he came home surly, muttering to himself, or breathless and sweaty, grateful to be home. He could be fun—laughing and joking, waving a wad of money and eager to take Steffi out for a good time—and when that happened, Bobbie could see why the prettiest girl around had gone for him. He always had jokes ready for them, the kind with nasty punchlines that made Bobbie cringe, jokes that made fun of sick people, gay people, black people. Such as, "What did the Zen Buddhist say to the hot dog vendor?"

Bobbie said she didn't know.

"'Make me one with everything.'" Aaron threw back his head and howled. He had a deep, resonant voice, a mirthful laugh that made Bobbie think he should have gone into broadcasting instead of whichever racket he was currently in.

At about seven o'clock one evening, the Wellmans entered the Claymore Inn, both of them dusting bits of frost from their coats. They sat in Bobbie's section. Mr. Wellman, a handsome man, had strong features and a stocky build; his wife was a pretty woman just now starting to lose her looks. Bobbie decided that

Wil was a comfortable cross between them. She looked after them well, perhaps at the expense of other guests, and eavesdropped but heard nothing about Wil. Finally, while serving them coffee, she asked, "You're Wil's parents, right? How's he doing?"

Mr. Wellman, after shooting his wife a look that Bobbie could scarcely decipher, replied, "Wil is keeping busy and doing well."

Bobbie nodded and offered them a nervous smile. "Well, that's terrific. Be sure to tell him I said hi." She retreated from the table, wanting to believe Mr. Wellman's lie.

THAT DECEMBER, STEFFI became pregnant. Bobbie was shocked but not surprised. Who could picture Steffi as a mother? Steffi showed up for her shifts but was so lazy that the manager fired her. By summer, she was a behemoth. She and Aaron shared an apartment over a coin laundry whose noisy appliances were audible whenever Steffi opened her windows. Their apartment, such it was, contained scavenged pieces of furniture, an ancient puny stove and refrigerator, and a bathroom with a rusty faucet and peeling tile. "Aaron hates it," Steffi said. "He wants to build us a house on his land." Aaron had a parcel of Claymore land he claimed was his own, big enough for his dream. "He wants to build the best disco in the Bay Area. Or a house. He can't get a bank loan for either."

From the way Aaron talked, Bobbie believed that he felt lucrative business opportunities swarmed about like flies and mosquitoes.

Their apartment was comfortable enough in the mornings when the fresh valley breeze blew in. But the afternoons were torturous. Bobbie stayed away whenever she thought Aaron might be home. She cringed at the thought of him there with Steffi, hunched over their sticky Formica table, bragging about getting the better of one guy or griping about being ripped off by someone else. But on one afternoon, Steffi had called and begged her to drive over. Bobbie found her sitting on the edge of the bed, black hair sticking out in all directions, stomach huge. "I'm all knocked up, darlin'," she said.

"Looks like." Bobbie looked around the small

apartment. An oscillating fan blew hot air on them. "I can't believe you rented a place without air conditioning. How do you cope?"

Steffi shrugged. "Just think cool thoughts." Then, "I guess now my old man can't pimp me out to *Playboy*." Earlier in their relationship, Aaron, full of get-rich-quick ideas, wanted to take Polaroids of Steffi in the nude and send them off to Hefner's magazine. "Bobbie, have you seen such great tits? And how about that ass?" Bobbie, who had seen Steffi nude a few dozen times, had to agree: She was a spectacular beauty. Good enough for *Playboy*, certainly. Maybe even good enough for Hollywood. But now it was too late, and Aaron was probably blaming Steffi for that missed opportunity.

"So," Bobbie was saying, "what can I do for you *right now*?"

"Got your car? Get me the hell out of here."

Bobbie helped Steffi down the stairs and into her Pinto. "Where to?"

"Anywhere. Just drive. Get us a couple of beers, too."

"We're underage, and you shouldn't drink while

pregnant."

"Just do it, O.K.?"

So Bobbie pulled into the mall, walked into the Liquor Locker and bought two tall cans of Budweiser with out being carded. "Yummy," Steffi murmured, pressing the ice-cold can to her forehead. They got onto the highway, kept the windows rolled down and let the wind whip through their hair.

"Yuck!" Steffi pinched her nose. "Who farted?"

Bobbie laughed. "That smell comes from the oil refinery up there in the hills."

"Does it *have* to stink that bad?"

"Afraid so. If you want to turn crude oil into gasoline, you're going to have that odor."

"Reminds me of our bathroom after Aaron's taken a dump."

Bobbie guffawed. "Wanna go back yet?"

"Hell no."

Steffi instructed Bobbie to drive out to the north end of town, where several housing projects were under construction.

"What's there?" Bobbie wanted to know.

"I'll show you when we get there."

The north end, neglected for decades, had undergone development: Houses, trees, parks. People had finally discovered Claymore. As they reached Yolanda Avenue, Steffi hollered, "Here! Turn here!"

Bobbie pulled into what was mostly a smooth dirt parking lot. She stopped in front of a housing development that so far was little more than sheets of plywood nailed together.

"Kill the engine," said Steffi.

Bobbie did as told. "Well...?"

"Just sit tight."

Bobbie sighed and tapped on her thigh. In a moment, Wil Wellman appeared from behind the plywood. He wore jeans, boots, a toolbelt and no shirt. He had a tan now, and a better torso.

"What the—?"

Steffi smirked. "Lookin' good, huh?"

"How did you know he was back?"

"I know people who know people. Now, get his attention and send him over to say hi."

"Like hell," Bobbie said with a big, nervous swallow.

"I didn't ask you, I told you. *Do it.*"

So Bobbie did. She got out of the car, hurried up to Wil and said, breathless, "Come with me. There's someone who wants to see you."

He shielded his eyes with his hand, looking in the direction of the car, then smiled thanks at Bobbie. He took a moment, then said, "Bobbie Dyer."

"I'm flattered," she said, not knowing what to do with her hands. She watched as Wil hustled over to Steffi, his toolbelt jiggling, as, overhead, a few clouds scudded across the blue horizon.

LATER ON, BOBBIE wondered why Steffi wanted Wil to see her looking that way: Hair messy, clothes wrinkled, stomach huge with a bellyful of baby. But Steffi wasn't like other people, and Bobbie leaned against the plywood and watched as Wil peered down into the car and answered questions as Steffi fired them at her.

Her baby was born two weeks premature, while Aaron was in Nevada. Bobbie, expecting to be called any day to rush over and deliver Steffi to the hospital, heard nothing and wondered about the silence. Lynne, reading the *Times*, pointed to an item and said, "Isn't she the beautiful lazy girl you used to work with? She was married to that cocky guy who was sure he was gonna strike it rich?"

Bobbie looked: "Discharged from Claymore General: Mrs. A. Betts and son."

Steffi stood waiting at the top of the stairs, in a tattered bathrobe. She looked dreadful, as if recovering from major surgery rather than childbirth. Bobbie could hear the rumble of washers from downstairs.

"Why didn't you call me?" Bobbie asked. "How did you get to the hospital...?"

Steffi waved her off. "Just don't rag on me, OK?"

The baby was sleeping in the bassinet. His eyes were large and round, his color pink and caramel, like his mother's. "His name is Elijah. Don't make fun of it, OK?"

"Elijah is a wonderful name." Better than Bobbie, she thought.

Steffi sighed and shook her head. Then she pulled off her bathrobe and faced Bobbie. "Have a look."

Her breasts, once so gorgeous, were now grotesque; they stuck straight out in the saddest way, full of blue veins. Her nipples looked red and raw, ravaged, leaking discharge.

Bobbie swallowed, forced herself to look up at Steffi's face, then shrugged. She could think of nothing to say.

"What does Aaron think of all this? Where is he?" she finally asked .

"Beats me. He's still in Nevada, I guess."

Oh, no, Bobbie thought. Wil.

LYNNE WORKED AT the Inland Valley Department of Motor Vehicles. At home, she wanted serenity—she hurt all over, she'd spent the entire day dealing with assholes, she just wanted dinner and a few peaceful hours of TV. Bobbie said fine. But, night after night, Lynne grew bored with TV and its canned laughter. She sat on the sofa, sipping a glass of Blush Chablis, and called out her questions or remarks to Bobbie.

"Didn't hear you," Bobbie often had to say.

One evening, the phone rang. Wil was calling.

"Who's callin' this late?" Lynne called out.

"It's still early," Bobbie yelled, dragging the phone out of the kitchen and into the hallway.

"I don't know what to do," Wil said without saying hello. At first, she didn't even know it was him.

She pictured him out by the construction site, shirtless, muscular, manly. Now he sounded like a petulant child, calling Bobbie and expecting her to make it all better.

"I think about going back to M.I.T. and I get panic attacks. Maybe engineering isn't for me."

Why are you dumping this on me? she wanted to ask. She listened as he moaned. Where were his big-shot friends? She supposed she should be flattered that he was calling *her* for empathy.

"My father pushed me into M.I.T. I think I should just stay here and work."

"Bad idea," she said.

"Why?"

"Because you're better than that. An M.I.T. education is a very special thing. You have to take advantage of the opportunities you get." She nearly added, "You're better than *us*."

After several moments of silence, Wil said, "I tried calling Steffi, but her old man answered. I hung up."

"Well, he has a right to be there. I'm not sure why you want to speak to her, anyway. You guys have sort of gone your separate ways."

"Bobbie, I'd like to see you."

"Sure, one of these days—"

"How about right now?"

"No, it's late and—"

But of course she got into her car and drove out to the Denny's on Valley Road. Wil sat waiting for her and waved as she entered the restaurant. He wore a denim shirt and jeans. He looked to Bobbie like an actor playing a construction worker in a commercial.

"I've changed my mind," he said after getting up and hugging her hello. "This place isn't private enough."

So they got into his van and drank cans of King Cobra malt liquor. Bobbie felt thirsty most of the time and drank it down with gratitude. She watched Wil pucker his lips as he tried to figure out what he wanted to say to her, how he wanted to say it and what he wished to withhold.

Finally he spoke. "See, if I chose to stay here and keep doing construction, he would get me fired. He knows people, he's owed favors."

"You mean your father?"

He nodded. "Don't you think it's wrong for him to stick his nose into my personal business?"

"Because he wants you to stop hammering nails and go back to M.I.T.? A degree from that place will get you a great job, and you're gifted enough to get that degree. I think your father knows that."

"He's just being selfish and pushy." He started up his van and drove while he talked, not looking at her. He cruised up and down the main drag—now it was close to midnight. Bobbie rolled down her window and closed her eyes as the wind whipped her face. She still felt buzzed from the alcohol. Wil had weighed his options so many times, told himself and her the pros and cons that he now seemed to have paralyzed himself with indecision. But he still hadn't gotten to why M.I.T. had freaked him out. He'd breezed through Claymore High—and maybe that was the problem. At M.I.T., they'd made him *work*, and for the first time in his life he'd been in danger of flunking out. Was *that* the problem?

She turned to him and said, "You need to go back to M.I.T. and kick some ass." She smiled at the sound of that. She wanted to add, "Grow up, Wil."

BOBBIE GOT THROUGH to Wil that evening. A few months later she received a postcard of the campus with a simple message, "Keepin' busy," scrawled on the back in Wil's hand.

As fall deepened, Bobbie felt grateful for the end of summer, of its unremitting heat and all those nights she and her mother had spent in sleeping bags with the air conditioning on, all for the purpose of getting a good night's sleep. On her nights off, she babysat for Aaron and Steffi. She loved playing with Elijah, holding him, making him laugh by contorting her face. The apartment, uninsulated, became refrigerated in the winter, but Bobbie could live with that easily enough. The lights were undependable, the hot water went cold as often as not. Steffi and Aaron had no TV and seldom read books, so Bobbie brought over paperbacks she'd borrowed from the public library. She sat beside the sleeping baby and slogged through the books she thought she should read—*Crime and Punishment, Dubliners, The Price of the Ticket.* "Those books are better than sleeping pills," Steffi had told her.

One evening, Bobbie got worried. The clock said one o'clock, then two, and Steffi and Aaron were still away. After giving Elijah a bottle and putting him back down to sleep, Bobbie went to the window and looked outside, telling herself that in two minutes she was going to call the cops. But she spotted Aaron's truck in the driveway, and when hurried down the stairs, she discovered Steffi in the driver's seat, slumped over unconscious. "Come *on*, you've got to wake up and get it together," Bobbie said, pulling her friend out of the truck. Steffi pawed at the air, slapping Bobbie's face.

Aaron had got into a wreck, she said. He hit something, a car or a bear, maybe.

And where had he gone to now? Beats me, she muttered.

"Get on upstairs," Bobbie said. "You're too heavy to carry. Let's go."

Steffi nodded and stood straight up. It took them the longest time, but they made it, and Bobbie putt Steffi to bed. Afraid of leaving Elijah alone with his mother, Bobbie curled up on their sofa under half a dozen blankets. Hours later, she awoke to the sound of Steffi vomiting in the bathroom. She wanted to fix them some breakfast, but Steffi said no, she just wanted to sleep. Bobbie wrapped up Elijah and took him for a walk. The morning was perfect for her— cold and clear. She walked around Claymore's modest downtown, hoping to encounter a friend or acquaintance so she could show off the baby and enjoy the compliments (as if such compliments were somehow meant for *her*, too). On the way back to Steffi's, she took a long look at Aaron's truck and couldn't find any dents. What happened last night? she asked herself. Then she decided she didn't want to know.

"Hello, stranger. Do you still live here?" Lynne asked. Bobbie, tempted to answer her with a snotty retort, just shrugged and said, "I've been busy." She fed a sheet of paper into her manual typewriter and began writing a letter to Wil. (She had always liked the impersonal quality of typewritten documents, liked how it made the words look more intelligent, too.) She pecked out two paragraphs about nonsense, read them over, threw them away. She was careful not to say anything about Steffi, Aaron or their baby.

Then, on one spring evening, Wil called.

"You're calling from M.I.T., I hope," she said.

"'Fraid so."

"Good to know. It must be pretty late out there."

"What's Steffi up to?" he asked. "How is she?"

"Not a whole lot different from the last time we spoke about her."

"How did she feel about me? What did she think of us? Did she say anything about it?"

Oh no you don't. "You sure you're all right? You sound totally full of stress."

"Me? I'm OK. Just keeping busy and trying to keep up." Then, "You know, sometimes I think that the dumbest guy here is smarter than I am."

"You know that's not true. Want some good advice?"

"Always."

"Keep your mind on your studies and don't think about Steffi. She's ancient history. She doesn't exist for you anymore."

Bobbie made a point of not telling Steffi that Wil had called.

A few weeks after that, she went to Steffi's and saw her friend wearing oversized sunglasses. She had tripped and fallen, she said, banging herself in the eye. Maybe she was getting older and needed to have her vision checked.

"You need to be more careful," Bobbie said. "What if you had fallen while you were carrying the baby...?"

Steffi's widened her mouth into her biggest, brightest, most contemptuous smile. "Yes, Mom, I'll do that."

EASTER FINALLY ARRIVED, but Bobbie thought it still didn't feel that much like spring. They went to an outdoor Easter service and stood on the colorless, hard dry ground. Bobbie hadn't yet made up her mind about Christianity—too many miracles, too much violence—so she let her mind wander as the preacher spoke. She thought that a man nailed to a cross was a repulsive symbol for a religion. She hugged herself and wondered why she had put on such thin clothing. After the service, they had cookies and coffee. A few of the others came by and squeezed their arms. "Nice to see you two here," they said.

Towards the end of the service, people began to speak up, mostly about the optimism that spring confers. Even Lynne had a few words. I hope they don't want to speak, Bobbie thought, because I really, really have nothing to say. But then she looked at Lynne, who gave her the slightest shake of the head, letting her off the hook.

But she still had that feeling of being expected to speak or hear. That evening, as if she had been prepared for it, she saw Wil. He was alone, wearing an old overcoat, walking fast under the tall trees on Epp Street, a few blocks from Steffi's place. Plenty of red remained in the sky, a band starting to dissolve into pink. Bobbie wished it would stay that way forever.

"What are you doing? Where are you going?" she called out as she slowed down.

"Don't worry about it," he said.

But she did, and she guessed what he was up to. In fact, it was worse than she had guessed. He'd simply dropped out of M.I.T.—no, he hadn't even troubled himself to fill out the withdrawal forms—and was living in an old van down by Sutter River, a part of the valley that remained mostly desolate.

Bobbie and Wil worked something out: Instead of babysitting for Steffi and Aaron on her nights off, she now took Elijah on epic walks so that Wil could spend a few hours each day with Steffi. Why did she play along with Steffi and Wil's silly game? "Can't you at least do it in the van or go to a hotel?" she'd nearly asked, but chickened out. Steffi had that way of closing in on you and making you look at how the surgeon had reshaped her nose. Bobbie didn't like it; the tiny, straight nose just didn't go with Steffi's big, haunting eyes and generous, pink-lipped mouth. So Bobbie kept quiet and took the baby out for another walk, making sure to be nowhere in sight when Wil arrived. She hated to see that leering, ready-for-some-loving look that would overtake his face (probably, she admitted, because it wasn't for her). Also, how could any of them know that Aaron wouldn't suddenly materialize, angry and cursing as he barged in on his wife and her lover? What would happen then? Bobbie didn't think Aaron would punch it out with Wil. Aaron, for all his bragging and flexing, struck Bobbie as cowardly. He knew Wil could take him in two minutes if it came down to a fight. Anyway, Bobbie decided she'd had enough. She would just say no.

But of course she kept saying yes. She went back upstairs and came down with Elijah, murmuring, "Beautiful boy." After her walk, she returned and stood outside Steffi's door, sweating in the valley heat, listening for the familiar moans and giggles, hoping they were done for the day. She held her breath as she pushed open the door, and exhaled with gratitude if she saw Wil in his jeans, sitting at the Formica table, shirtless and winded. Steffi might still be in bed, the drenched sheets covering half of her, breasts or butt sticking out.

"You're too good to me," Steffi would say in

Bobbie's direction. That was the closest she ever came to saying thanks.

Bobbie, fed up, sometimes changed Elijah in silence and left without even nodding at either of them. Later, she asked herself in disgust: Why do I let these people take advantage of me? What's in it for me? But on some days, she got her reward. Wil, seated at the table, grabbed Bobbie by the waist and pulled her onto his lap; she blushed and beamed as he rested his chin on her shoulder and whispered to her. A few feet away, Steffi splashed around in the bathroom and sang to herself. In front of them, she pulled on wrinkled, stained clothes over her long, flaccid, caramel-colored body, acting as if all this—cheating on her husband while her best friend cared for her child—were a perfectly acceptable way of life.

"You hungry?" Wil asked Bobbie. "Let's go eat." First, though, he had to hunt around for his shirt and sneakers.

Steffi stood there, running a hand through her hair. "I was just thinking," she told them, "that it would be so nice if you two weren't here."

"She's kicking us out, Bobbie," said Wil. He

gathered up his shirt and shoe, put them on in a hurry. He then kissed Elijah on the forehead. "Let's go. My ride's down the alley."

At his van, he unlocked the passenger's door and tossed aside some textbooks and stapled-together mimeographed sheets. One of the books was called *Numerical Heat Transfer and Fluid Flow*. "Pretty esoteric stuff," Bobbie said, picking it up. "But it doesn't weigh very much."

"Yeah, and it cost a small fortune." He started up the van and threw it into reverse.

Bobbie rolled down her window, enjoying the spring breeze but aware of the traces of summer heat it carried. She wondered why she, a native Californian, had never learned to cope well in hot weather. He drove to Denny's, the same place where they were going to meet up earlier. He didn't care now who saw him, or saw him with her. That was a lifetime ago. He looked to her as if he hadn't eaten in days, but he did eat. Sandwiches, onion rings, a gooey caramel dessert and plenty of coffee. With Steffi absent, Bobbie had his full attention.

"So," she said, "tell me about chemical

engineering." She smiled at him, urging him to talk about what he liked and knew. She was ready to learn.

"Lend me your pen," he said. She nodded and handed him the felt-tip pen in her shirt pocket. He pulled a bunch of napkins out of the dispenser and filled them with drawings. She knew he was dumbing it down for her sake, but she still had to concentrate to follow him. She watched, listened, smiled. His father knew him better than he thought; the old man had been smart to push him in that direction.

She reached over and touched his hand as he finished a sketch. "You, uh, could spend the night with me." She looked at him, head tilted, as if she'd spoken in a language that he maybe didn't understand. "You know?"

"I know," he said with a smile. She sensed he felt slightly surprised but mostly flattered. Of *course* he knew he could have her, and the idea wasn't so ludicrous, either. He looked past her, through the window, and nodded the tiniest bit.

WAS SHE IN love with him? She wasn't even sure she knew what being in love was all about, how it felt.

Now she felt the need to mature, to start making specific plans and acting upon them. *Time to grow up*, an inner voice told her. She got mad at herself—she thought that she could just hang back and let adulthood and success and fulfillment wash over her like a spring rain. She got mad at Wil, too, for squandering his M.I.T. time. She also hated herself for spending so much time worrying about what might happen if Aaron had caught Steffi with Wil. That was *their* problem; why should she care? If Aaron did catch Wil and Steffi together, he wouldn't pick that fight Bobbie was sure he would lose; no, he would just wait till Wil got dressed and left, then Aaron would slap Steffi around their apartment for an hour. Steffi had a banged-up quality about her—nicks and cuts, unhealed bruises. But she'd made it all work for her, like scars on fine leather. Bobbie now saw Steffi as an aging movie beauty, with marks no plastic surgeon could erase, but she was still Steffi, full of presence and sparkle. She'd lied to Bobbie a hundred times, too…and when had they ever had a conversation of any consequence? Wasn't it usually just Steffi bitching about her lot in life or bullying Bobbie for time-consuming, inconvenient favors, as if Bobbie had nothing better to do?

Bobbie seldom went straight home after work now. Instead, after changing out of her white blouse and black skirt, she drove for hours and covered miles, listening to the radio. The local stations crackled with static, but she could get the major Bay Area stations clearly. Occasionally she would get on the westbound freeway and keep on going until she reached San Francisco. Determined to overcome her ignorance of the world around her, she tuned into KGO, the top-rated talk station. She finally parked in a residential neighborhood, at the top of a hill, and gazed at the glittering skyline while she listened to the host and callers going back and forth on the issues of the day: Vietnam, Watergate, the lessons America (should have) learned from the Arab oil embargo of 1973. Bobbie paid the closest attention, forced herself to take it all in, and managed not to think of Steffi for minutes at a time.

One evening, she decided to drive into San

Francisco, then thought better of it and got off the freeway. Back in Claymore, she crossed the Miller Bridge, slowed down so that the crumbling blacktop wouldn't destroy her tires, then crept along a sandy road that led to the edge of the river. I won't find him here, she told herself, and even if I do, what will I say to him. But she spotted his van soon enough. A small, feeble fire struggled a dozen feet away. The side doors were open and his legs hung out. She sauntered all the way up to him and put her hand on his knee. He looked up at her and smiled. "You're late. I've been expecting you for a while now."

"I should have showered first," she said. "I smell like a wild animal."

"No, you don't. *I* do."

"Tell me about this. Why do you live in a van by the river?" Then she added, "No, I don't want to hear about it."

"Shut up and come give me a kiss," he told her.

She nodded and climbed onto his lap. She kissed him as best she could, even though her lips were dry and thin. She wished she had Steffi's lips, full and pink, just too kissable.

Wil put his hands under her shirt, caressing her back. "Full speed ahead?"

"You talk too much," she said, pushing him so that he lay on his back. She sat astride him, and his hands made their way up to her cheeks and stayed there for the longest time. Was her face that fascinating to him, or was he just not that interested in the rest of her?

"Get me naked," she said. "Before I say no."

He had an air mattress underneath him that made little gasps like a dying man. The overhead light was too dim for her to see much, but she noticed a couple of knapsacks, also a pile of bunched-up shirts and jeans he probably hadn't washed in weeks. She could smell a mountain of debris—food and candy-bar wrappers, stale old beer cans. Typical guy, she thought—happy enough living in his own filth.

Presently they were mostly naked. Bobbie had often thought that the best way to be with a man was standing up, in an embrace. But the Bobbie she saw in those standing-up embraces was not her but a far prettier woman her imagination had conjured up, with better curves and clearer skin. Here in the van, he couldn't see that well, and he probably had his eyes closed, anyway. Wil lay there, doing what he had done so many times before. Maybe he was thinking of Steffi.

"I'm too…" She felt like putting herself down, soliciting praise from him, but then decided against it. He was with her now, inside of her. She was good enough.

Still, she flashed on Steffi in the Claymore High shower, all eyes and breasts, tummy as tight as a drum. "Having a good time?" Bobbie asked Wil, meaning to sound clever but instead somehow making fun of them.

He grunted a little. She took that as a yes.

"Too much fun," she said. She didn't feel the earth move, oceans part, mountains crumble. But it was *fun*, it felt *good*. She could have kept it going for hours.

"Gotta change positions," Wil said, and sat up. Bobbie did, too, and smacked her head on the overhead light. They both heard it crack; it sounded like a firecracker had gone off.

"Damn!" Wil said. "I'm so sorry. Are you all right?"

"No," she said. "It hurts like hell."

He groped around, found a bandanna and pressed it over the top of her head. "Keep it like this. You're gonna need stitches. Gotta get you to a hospital."

She groaned. She felt covered with gooseflesh. Suddenly she felt cold, sleepy. They both struggled into their clothes and Wil crawled into the driver's seat. Bobbie got into the passenger's seat and laughed.

"I can't imagine what you think is funny," he said.

"You didn't even...we didn't finish." Then, "What'll we tell them at the hospital?"

"The truth: that you hurt your head."

Then she sat under the merciless glare of the emergency room at Claymore General, wincing and sighing as they stuck a needle into her arm, shaved off a small patch of hair and sewed up the tiny tear in her scalp. The doctor, a lanky, bearded younger man, asked her little about her accident and frowned at disbelieve the lie she spat out. Bobbie was a very young woman and this was California in the late Seventies; the doctor was probably relieved that she wasn't another overdose. Wil waited in a black padded chair down the hallway. She could see him when the examination room's door was open—he sat there, chin on his hands, probably mentally reliving their encounter in the van and how he could have made it all work out differently. Then the door was closed, the doctor treated her, and when the door was open again, Wil was gone.

She hurried out into the parking lot and found him leaning against his van. The sky was very dark now, the breeze warm; the red lights high up in the distance comforted Bobbie, as they always had. She liked the hills of the valley, too, the Wild West feeling they gave her.

"Sorry I left you," Wil was saying. "I just can't stand hospitals. They make me sick."

Bobbie laughed. "I have to get back to my car."

"You're in no condition to drive."

"But I have to get my car. I'll be all right."

He nodded. "It's not that far."

They stayed silent all the way back to the river. Bobbie looked up, saw the stars pulsating in the stars, wished she could go back to the hospital parking lot and stare at the red lights for a few more minutes. She wanted to say she was sorry, but knew nothing had been her fault and Wil would get angry—she was blaming herself for something he believed was *his* fault—as if fault, like property, had an owner.

The sky remained deep gray and the world quiet as Bobbie let herself into her apartment.

"Who dat?" Lynne called out in a sleepy voice.

"Just me." Bobbie went into the bathroom, her scalp sore, head buzzing with pain. She took a couple of Tylenol 3s and sat on the edge of the tub, wondering if she should take a bath. A couple of minutes later, she entered her bedroom and lay down, sure that as soon as the painkillers kicked in she would drift off into a long, restful sleep.

But no; she woke a short time later, still in her jeans and T-shirt, mind chaotic with thoughts, heart thundering in her ears. Morning hadn't arrived yet, but the sky had turned into a lighter shade of gray. A brisk wind that started rattling the trees, causing a loose telephone wire to slap the side of Bobbie's apartment.

She needed to go back to him. They had too many things to say to each other. She needed to speak to him, and to hear him say things to her.

She put on her shoes and socks, crept out of her room and listened at Lynne's door. Hearing nothing but Lynne's heavy breathing, she opened the door a crack and saw her mother tangled up in the blankets and sheets, limbs askew, paperback novels and reading glasses strewn about. Lynne craved sleep and seemed unable to get enough of it. Bobbie saw it as a colossal waste of time.

Bobbie pulled her car out onto the street. A Valley Gas and Electric truck crept along, the only thing on the road besides her. She found a sort of safety in not being alone out there, felt a bit of disappointment as the lumbering vehicle with its yellow roof light faded into the distance She headed towards the river till she reached the dirt road, then killed her lights before she reached him. She found his van, exactly where it had been, except that the fire was out, kicked apart so that she could never have guessed it had been there. She threw open the back doors and crawled in, feeling around but saying nothing. Then she figured out he wasn't in there.

She spotted him down at the river's edge, his legs dangling over the embankment. The big river ran past, indifferent to his presence. He sat huddled over in a heavy jacket. He probably hasn't slept well in days, she thought. He looked cold and afraid, nothing like the stylish, cocky man-boy she'd admired a few years earlier. She wanted to run up to him, hooting and giggling; but the next moment, she felt a mature, adult self-control—it overtook her, made her feel womanly and in charge. Hours earlier, scrambling out of Wil's van, she'd flashed back on the good deeds she'd done for all of those people—even Elijah—and it occurred to her that she'd been put there for a reason, to be there for them, to be the one they all depended on. As the sun rose, the extraordinariness of the night before dimmed into another mundane morning. That's how it is, as Lynne often said—you'll just have to deal with it.

The morning wind blew through her hair as she walked towards him, calling out his name. She had to sit down next to him before he looked at her and nodded. She rubbed his leg and said, "What a long, strange trip it's been."

He nodded. "And it's only just begun."

She looked him straight in the eye. "Don't go over

there ever again."

He wasn't interested in talking about that. She wanted him to, but knew he would rather sit there, with or without her, and stare up at the morning sky.

"I mean it, Wil. Stay away. There's nothing for you over there."

"I can't promise you that," he said.

"Of *course* you can."

She let him think about that for a little while as she sat back and watched a boat cruise along the river. A couple of people stood at the front, with a dog between them. The dog looked in Bobbie and Wil's direction, shot them a bark, lost interest in them and sniffed his human companions. Across the river, trees bent and swayed from the valley wind. Even in this, the first light of morning, Bobbie saw a lively glow in the leaves, the promise of a new day and the countless opportunities it presented. Yes, Bobbie thought, a new day, a gift from Mother Nature. She leaned over and kissed Wil's cheek. Very soon, he would understand what she wanted of him. They were stuck with each other, together for the long haul—it sounded odd to say it that way, but Bobbie knew she was right.

PAPPY'S PET

Pappy liked Cookie the best. He always said that girls in the sticks were as useless as nipples on a boy. He had three girls, and Artie died in infancy. Pappy always wanted a boy, and when Cookie, number four, came along, he got what he wanted, sort of. A tomboy, she followed him everywhere. She went out to the garage and hung out with the mechanics. They taught her to fix cars. Cookie was the type, you just had to show her once and she learned it right away. Soon, if a car broke down, Cookie could take over and repair it. All I knew about cars was stick the key in and hit the gas. At sixteen, I said, "Pappy, I want a car." He tossed me the keys and said, "See that old subcompact, Goof? It's yours." He'd nicknamed me Goof. I knew he loved me and his other girls, but he hated females in general, thus my nickname. Pappy was always kind to me, and although he was a handsome man and the ladies liked him, deep down inside he really despised women. He was just awful to Mum. He would hang out with trashy women and buy them expensive gifts, then go home and tell Mum about it. She would get so enraged she would scream or faint or burst into tears. My sisters and I would have to take her into the back room of the store and put a cold compress on her forehead till she recovered. In the kitchen, while fixing supper, she would scowl because of how cruel he was to her.

So Pappy gave me an old Honda he'd left parked outside near a huge tree. It looked and smelled ancient, but it ran O.K.. Well, Barbie Kennett and I took it out for a drive on Sundown Avenue. I didn't even know what I didn't know about driving, so I accidentally slammed the vehicle into a fire hydrant. She and I walked home through brutal Sundown heat; we could see the air shimmer above the road's surface. People forget how hot British Columbia can get in the summer. At home I told Pappy about my misadventure and he just shrugged and told one of his mechanics to take me out in a Ford—Pappy sold Fords—and teach me to drive. Once I got so I could drive without killing anyone or totaling the car, I got a new Ford. Pappy sometimes did nice things like that for us. When Reenie told him she wanted to learn tennis, he personally built her a tennis court and bought her some fancy, pretty tennis whites, too. After a while she got bored with it and moved on to other interests.

Cookie learned tennis in ten minutes and soon could beat everyone in the valley. She could take on all the men, but with Pappy she would let him win even though he had no gift for tennis.

Pappy had a punching bag in the basement. He loved to pound on it and show off for those who cared to watch. He let the little kids use it, too, and some of them got pretty good at it. Pappy liked kids and knew how to get along with them, so they thought he was a good Gus. I could punch the bag, too, but Cookie would kick and punch it like a professional. She could take any of the boys in two minutes if it came down to a fight, as it sometimes did. She kept on that way till she was thirteen and got her first period and boobies. Those changes in her body, which should have surprised her not at all, quite overwhelmed her.

Pappy played the fiddle and danced and called square dances. Everyone liked him. He could have run for mayor. He had Mum pack us lunches so he could take us out to swim in one of the nearby lakes. In the winter he would buy us skis and take us out to the mountains to enjoy the glorious Canadian snow. Mum didn't join us; she stayed at the store but wished us a good time.

The four of us were pretty girls, but Cookie was stunning. She had dirty blonde hair and emerald-colored eyes and a big blonde smile. She looked like a cover girl or movie star but wore no makeup and kept her hair short. Still, people stared at her and licked their lips. By then Pappy was drunk all the time, losing his money, buying his girlfriends presents he couldn't afford. When he ran out of money, he stole some from Mum. One time he came home gooned, demanded money from Mum, but she wouldn't give him any, so he pulled out his revolver and pointed it at her temple. Mum was pregnant with Sunny then and very nearly miscarried her. Pappy called Mum the filthiest names he could think of and he slapped her around like she was a dog that had misbehaved. That was a horrible thing, but Pappy was Pappy and Mum was Mum and that was life at our house.

When Pappy pulled his gun on Mum, that was the only time I ever thought he would kill her. I remember the afternoon when all of us girls had to manage the store while Mum lay in bed fretting over

Pappy's well-being while she gave birth to Sunny. Minutes after Mum had Sunny, Pappy came home looking worse than death. Some guys brought him home because he'd drunk way too much Canadian Comfort and was screaming that he couldn't see. The doctor said there was nothing left to do, and Pappy vomited when he wasn't screaming. He died four days later, and my sisters and I took care of him because Mum was busy taking care of Sunny and she no longer had any use for Pappy. He lay there and stretched out and died in the same bed where his daughter had just been born.

To tell the truth, I was the one who pretty much cared for Pappy, looked after Sunny and ran the store. I was the oldest of the sisters so it always seemed to be, "Let Goof take care of it."

Not long after Pappy's funeral a lawyer came to see Mum and said that we would lose all our property because Pappy had racked up so many unpaid debts. Mum got another lawyer and said that all she wanted was the store; if she could keep that, she would repay all that money, which amounted to just under $100,000. That seemed like a vast amount of money, but Mum worked and worked and paid it all back.

I would say that of all us girls, none of us got special treatment from Mum, but that changed when Sunny was born. She had curly hair and apple cheeks and dimples, and customers liked to come into the store so they could ooh and ahhh over the baby. Sunny seemed even prettier than Cookie because the little one was always dolled up and looking like a store-bought little princess. But whenever Cookie went to any trouble to look her best, well, she was just absolutely movie-queen stunning, with her dirty blonde hair and big green eyes and full pink lips. Just too damn beautiful.

When Cookie turned sixteen, the boys simply would not leave her be. She would not date them. She would play sports with them and clown around because she was still a tomboy who wasn't ready top give up her fun and games, but she wouldn't make out with them. Cookie had spells like Mum—that was about the only thing they had in common—and she would collapse onto her bed while we put cold packs on her forehead. It seemed strange for Cookie to get sick and need help—because she was so tough, doing without sleep and working harder than any man—but when she had spells she talked out loud to people who weren't there and heard things the rest of us couldn't hear. She told us Jesus was in the room and they spoke to each other. Her bad spells started right after she got her first period.

Everything Cookie did had to be perfect. At school she did the best because she wouldn't put her name on an assignment till it was the best ever. She was the valedictorian of her class and went off to college to study medicine. She came home for a visit one Christmas and told me all the men at college wanted to get her into bed. She said she had more important things to do than mess around with men. She had always been Pappy's pet and no other man could be to her what he had been. If you ever got up in her face about how Pappy smacked Mum or put his gun to her temple, she would walk away or get up in *your* face about how much Mum had failed Pappy. One time, Reenie started whining about Pappy's bad behavior, and after Cookie told her to shut up, she kept on about him until Cookie hauled off and knocked her cold with one punch. She broke Reenie's nose and it hardened crooked. Cookie fought like a man and hit you as hard as she could, which was plenty hard. She was voluptuous and ethereal—Bo Derek, but taller with green eyes—and in medical school whenever she got stressed out—which was most of the time—she gobbled up junk food from the vending machines. The next time she came home, she was so fat I almost didn't know it was her. We talked while she stripped to take a shower. I didn't know what to think of her pot belly, big fat bum and double chin. She seemed to like her new fat self just fine. Cookie was the first woman doctor in Sundown. Nobody was prouder of her than Mum; Mum said that if you were a woman, you owed it to yourself and the rest of womankind to get educated and fulfill your potential. Cookie won scholarships and went to Queen's University, which was where all the Canadian brainiacs went.

Mum sent me to secretary school, but then I was hanging out with Asa so I quit after a little while. Reenie married Horace and he was mostly good to her although he couldn't seem to keep his hands off of other women. Horace, a smart businessman, made a pile of money and moved them to Vancouver, so we didn't see much of them after that. Sunny married Jonas when she turned nineteen and he went into the military and came home from Afghanistan all shell-shocked. He left my sister for some tramp and Sunny kind of fell apart for a while. We had to look after her till she got her head back together and married Silvo. Becka, the second-oldest of us and, to me, the one most like Cookie, married her boyfriend Mack and moved to Seattle. Mum mostly ran the store, although by then she had grandkids she could boss around in there. Plus, her daughters were usually just a short distance away. Sunny seldom did much to help in the store or anywhere else. She was the opposite of Cookie. Sunny had hot pants for men; she went all crazy whenever one came by.

Mum used to stand behind the counter and chat with customers as they came in. That was part of the service; a few minutes with her if you wanted it. Whenever they spoke to her, she would stand there nodding and say, "How about that, eh?" No matter what they said, her reply would be, "How about that, eh?" She had a big body and sticks for legs. Mum had been pretty when young, and Pappy had been a handsome man, too, so when their daughters grew up to be cuties, everyone said we simply inherited our parents' good looks. Which I suppose we did.

Chasbo and I lived just across the street from the store. My husband, a wimp, rarely lasted more than a couple of weeks at any job. Whiny and full of complaints, he often saw Cookie for this or that medical complaint, real or imagined. He'd sit in her office beaming at his smart, amazing sister-in-law; she diagnosed his condition as loneliness and boredom. Cookie gave him sugar pills and told him to take one three times each day. Chasbo took the pills and instantly felt better. Cookie genuinely liked him and told him about religion and how he could enjoy life more if he accepted Jesus into his life. Cookie had become fascinated by religion after seeing and hearing Jesus and beginning menstruation all those years ago. When she entered the store one day and announced she had converted to Catholicism, Mum went bananas. We had been raised as Lutherans, and to her Catholicism was one step above atheism. Mum and Cookie raged at each other in the store, and I wondered for a moment if Cookie would pound her the way she did Reenie that time. A thunderstorm was happening at that moment and a lightning bolt hit a tree nearby and split it in half, as if God Himself was getting involved in Mum and Cookie's dispute. It scared me so much that I thought I would have a heart attack and die.

Mum always got unsettled during severe weather, and during this thunderstorm, while she and Cookie screamed at each other, Mum starting shaking. The electricity went out and I started lighting candles while Mum and Cookie argued, Mum acting as though converting to Catholicism was somehow a crime against God. The bad weather outside and the hostility inside got Mum rattled just the way she was that time Pappy drew his gun on her. It started to hail, and Cookie got so hot that she left in her Oldsmobile and Mum went upstairs to lie down and recover from their confrontation.

Soon after that we got a letter from Cookie saying that she had become a Catholic nun. More than a year later we received another letter from her. She had gone to Africa to work as a doctor serving the poorest of the poor. She said she was exactly where the Lord wanted her to be.

My husband wanted me to quit the Lutheran church and not go to church at all for a while, so I obeyed him. He worked here and there whenever this or that boss was willing to hire him. He collapsed and died one day in his early thirties. Just before he died, he said to me, "Goof, I've been sick since I can't remember when. I'm going off to a better place."

After Mum died, her health destroyed by a dozen ailments, Cookie wrote to the lawyer asking that Mum's money be used to buy medicine for the poor people in Africa. Becka talked the lawyer into doing as Cookie wanted. Becka and Cookie liked each other and Becka wrote to Cookie each month while Cookie was in Africa, telling her about life in Sundown with Mack. He and Becka had a happy life because he made good money and they had all the goodies they wanted. Becka wrote only about the good things and left out the bad things that happen to all people no matter where they live. Becka reminded Cookie of how the two of them had tricked that lawyer into sending Mum's money to the poor people in Africa. "Those poor people need it more than we do, eh?" she wrote.

On the day Sunny called to tell me that Becka had cancer, she just said, "Becka phoned me and said, 'The doctor said I've got breast cancer.'" That's what she said. Becka didn't seem too worried about it; she figured it was all part of God's plan for her. Mack fell apart; Becka and their kids were everything to him and he couldn't bear the idea of parting with her. They took her to the hospital for a mastectomy. After she returned home, she told me, "I've asked Jesus to make sure all my cancer is gone, so I believe I will be O.K." But then the cancer spread to her lungs, so they put her on oxygen but she died anyway. Her death was way worse than it sounds, and I hope nothing like that happens to me. I have diabetes, so I will probably keel over from a heart attack. My husband says a heart attack makes it seem like an elephant is sitting on your chest. The pain is severe, but it's over soon. Isn't that nice, the way most of us must suffer and die while we're here on this planet?

I was just as glad to see Becka's suffering end, but it upset me that Mack now had this huge hole in his life. He said he didn't want to remarry, but his kids said it would be nice to have a stepmom. Then his dog Ringo died and Mack went on a drinking binge. The rest of us stayed away from him while he was drunk. Our family has no patience with drink or drunks—Mum taught us that.

Soon Cookie came home from Africa in her nun's habit. She was pushing fifty by then and her looks had faded; her face was as gray as her hair. Life is sure difficult there, she told us, with poor food and nonstop work. "The harder we try, the less we accomplish," she said.

The Catholic Church gave her time off to come home and do whatever she needed, so right away she got Mack off booze and started me on insulin therapy. She didn't come home for Mum's funeral or Reenie's funeral, but aside from Pappy, Becka was her best friend so she flew home to say goodbye to our sister.

I said, "Cookie, it's lovely to see you but you look worse than a corpse. What's that all about?" She said that in Africa a huge cobra came slithering into her village and started biting people and animals. She grabbed its tail and tried to pull it away, like she'd seen on TV, but it just sort of whirled around and bit her, too. She told me her life and health had gone downhill since then. Anyway, she gave me a bunch of crap because of my bad diet and lack of exercise, and I told her that if the Good Lord, assuming He existed, wanted to take me home, I would be happy to go, and when I got to heaven, assuming it existed, would I be reunited with Chasbo, my first husband, or Wil, my second one? Cookie said she'd stopped believing in God. I said, "Cookie, you are a nun. What do you mean you don't believe in God?" She just laughed and shrugged and said her habit was just clothing and it didn't mean jackshit—God did not exist except in a lot of people's wishful thoughts. Once you die that's the end of you, and that's not necessarily a bad thing. But she took Mack to A.A. meetings and he stayed sober. He loved Cookie, always had and always would, even if she was just a haggard-looking, middle-aged broad by then. Although she pretended otherwise, she was going through a crisis of her own—she didn't belong back here in Sundown, and she sure didn't feel at home on the Dark Continent. She was all jokes and giggles, but Mack could tell she was hurting. As much as we all rallied around him, he just sort of gave up inside. Both his kids and his wife died before he did. His last words were to Cookie and me, on his deathbed. He said, "I'm sick of this bullshit," then he rolled over and died. I think that, deep down inside, what he really wanted was to marry Cookie. He would have asked her, if he'd thought there was any chance she'd say yes, which there wasn't, but he loved her that much.

There was this guy on a TV talk show who said that you could cure yourself of terminal illnesses by laughing, because your laughter produces hormones or whatever that fight the disease. He said you should watch the Three Stooges or Marx Brothers. Well, those stupid guys could never make *me* laugh hard enough to produce the right hormones, so I guess I'll just have to lay down and die when the time comes. Mack lost his wife, kid and dog one after another, and he couldn't recover from that. At A.A. he learned all that higher power stuff he chose to call God, and it helped him quit drinking and smoking.

One evening Cookie drove by to see me and caught me eating junk food. She went up one side of me and down the other; I said, "Cookie, you can get in my face all you want about it, but I'm gonna eat whatever I like. That's just how it is."

She shook her head in disgust. Then we drove out to see Mack. He hugged us both hard and I thought he would cry as he squeezed Cookie. We sat in the living room and he went on and on for hours. Late at night, when my leg cramps keep me awake, I think of Mack and Becka and their kids all up in heaven except for Pappy, who pissed Him off once too often.

My doctor for most purposes now is Cookie, which is fine with me. I've got a hundred things wrong with me, which according to her is fairly common as we age. Sometimes I just have to tough it out and endure the pain; at those times I lay in bed with a picture of Jesus and pray for Him to take me, or at least to accept Cookie's soul when her time comes. She has done some wonderful things for God's crazy world, but only with His permission will she be welcomed into the Kingdom of Heaven.

Cookie quit the Catholic Church and used Becka's

money to start her own family medical practice. She sees patients, writes prescriptions and orders tests five days a week and at night goes out to dance and flirt with men. I saw her the other day and about the only thing left of her looks are her dazzling green eyes; her blonde hair is now a dull gray and her golden complexion is now pallid. I'm not sure she's a follower of Jesus; maybe during her years in Africa she got caught in the grip of Satan, although Jesus did look after a bunch of times, especially when she got bitten by that cobra. I believe that Satan, Prince of Darkness, rules this world, always looking for souls who will do his dirty deeds. But I always thought Cookie was just too smart to get mixed up with him.

Maybe Cookie's troubles happened mostly because of Pappy. She was his special girl, and I don't think that's always necessarily a good thing. I believe that all people can go to heaven if they accept the grace of God, but too many people are just unwilling to do such a thing. Cookie much of the time thought that Christianity is irrational, which it is, but maybe that heaven stuff is for real. Cookie had traveled too far and seen too many weird and awful things. She had gone to Africa and been bitten by a cobra. AIDS and Africa and snakebites were real to her; Christian theology was just a bunch of hocus-pocus. I've always lived my life believing in Christian theology but I've seen so much evil that I don't know what to think now. I hold the picture of Jesus and pray for Cookie and myself and all the wretched souls of this Earth. I say, "Jesus, come down now and save us from ourselves because we know not what we do!" When I say this the adult in me dies and I become a small child again. Many times I don't *really* believe that there is life after death—but it's a wonderfully comforting thought, just like when a preacher said to me, "After you die you will enter into the Kingdom of Heaven, and I'm sure you'll find it's quite magnificent." So I thought, 'Well, then, I sure have something to look forward to.'

I am getting on in years and need to say these things before I find out firsthand if there's a Kingdom of Heaven.

THE MAN FROM DREAM CITY

Andy Rae stared at the bathroom mirror, trying to remember who and where he was. He still felt out of sorts from that acid trip on Saturday night. He had double vision and his bones and nerves felt all buzzed and jangled. He then recalled that it was Monday morning and he was trying to get his shit together so he could go to school.

He told himself he'd been a fool to drop that acid, especially now that on Monday morning he still felt fucked up. He considered himself lucky not to be back in the psych ward. He opened a pill vial, shook out a couple of lithium tablets and choked them down. Then he smoked a Pall Mall and made a face in the mirror. Although small, he had a mean-looking face and when he chose to act crazy, people backed off. Andy paid little attention to the future; he figured it did not include him.

"Andy, I gotta go. Late for work. You were up half the night. Please take your meds. If you start another cycle, *I'll* go crazy."

Homeroom on Monday morning was never any fun,

but at least Liz Macfarlan was there, which was rare for her. Even though Andy had seen myriad porn movies on the Internet, he still felt that when it came to sex, he didn't even know what he didn't know. Damn, he sure wanted some of what Liz had on her chest and between her legs, and she knew it.

Liz wore skirts, patent-leather Mary Janes and lace-fringed anklets. She had a beautiful face, long, slender legs and firm, plump breasts. Goddamn! He flashed his best James Dean look as he slung his knapsack over his shoulder and followed her out the door when the bell rang.

She was maybe sixteen years old but in most ways Liz impressed Andy as being a grown woman. She carried herself in such an adult manner and he knew she dated a twenty-something guy who drove a Mustang. Andy guessed her parents pretty much just let her be. She surely banged her boyfriend a few nights per week and Andy envied him enormously.

As he followed Liz down the hallway, Andy daydreamed about her as Stef Jessman slammed into him. He didn't fully understand who was in his face as Jessman thumped him in the chest with a finger and said, "You're dead after school, goof!"

Andy blinked a few times and thought, *Shit! Why do I run my fuckin' mouth so much?* He had spray-painted obscenities all over Jessman's car, but he hadn't told anyone, not even Jewison on drug night. Or had he?

After class, Andy went to his locker and stuffed his English textbook inside it. Then he stepped over to Jewison's locker. Jewison had foolishly given Andy the combination to his locker, so Andy popped it open and took out Jewison's lunch, which, as always, was totally delicious, whereas Andy's mother prepared

142

consistently crappy lunches. Andy put his own inadequate lunch into Jewison's locker and devoured the good one. He was still mad at Jewison for selling him an old, useless tab of ecstasy for thirty dollars. He enjoyed gobbling up Jewison's tasty lunch but it only partly revived him.

In the cafeteria, Jewison, a tall, scrawny youth with hideous acne, opened his lunch bag and sneered at its contents. "Shitty lunch. No butter, no lettuce, bread isn't even fresh. She's got a growin' boy to feed. Why is she giving me shit for lunch?"

"Maybe she's puttin' you on a diet," said their buddy Payne.

"Doesn't your mum usually make good lunches?" Andy asked, trying to hide his smirk.

Jewison scowled. "Lately her lunches have been totally shitty. Gotta talk to her about it." He shook his head in disgust as he stuck the sorry-looking sandwich into the bag. "What are you lookin' at, dickhead?" he asked Andy.

"I'm lookin' at that awful sandwich your mum made you. What did she give you for dessert, a used Tampax? Hahaha!"

"What's the deal with you? Did you stop taking your meds?" Jewison asked.

Payne said, "Sometimes he goes off his lithium and starts acting weird." To Andy he said, "Do *Bad Boys* for us."

Andy nodded. "'My name is Gene Daniels. You can call me Mr. Daniels—I like that; don't call me anything else. In case you think you're hip, you're not; if you were, you wouldn't be here. The other inmates here are murderers, rapists, armed robbers and mental defectives, just like yourselves. You will be treated with respect if you treat others with respect. I suggest you stay cool and follow all the rules—'"

Payne and Jewison shook their heads. "Not so fuckin' loud. Everyone can hear you," said Payne.

"Better get back on your lithium or they'll throw your ass back in Oceanview," said Jewison.

Payne stood up. "You're a pain the ass when you go off your meds and act like an asshole. I'm not talkin' to you again."

Andy's English class was reading *The Confessions of Nat Turner.* He liked studying such a controversial novel. He .hated, and always struggled with, math and science, but he read fast and genuinely enjoyed literature. While at Oceanview, despite megadoses of psychiatric medications, Andy read a couple of huge novels each day—it was a great way to forget about the mental institution for a while and explore distant lands. In those pages he found options for a new life and ways to improve himself. Quality literature was his road to salvation. But once the shrink discharged him and sent him home he reverted to his old, foul ways.

After English class, Andy, remembering that Jessman had threatened to thrash him after school, gathered up his gear for gym class so he wouldn't have to go back to his locker, where Jessman would surely be waiting for him. After P.E., Andy went to the A&B Pool Hall to unwind before going to work.

Eddie Bonzai sat in the manager's office with the door open, drumming his fingers on his desktop. Andy put on his uniform before the manager knew he was there. Eddie, an obese alcoholic pedophile, spent countless hours sitting in shopping malls watching the children walk by. When he saw Andy, he smiled and said, "So, Andy boy! How was your weekend? Did you pump some pussy?"

"I always do. My weekend sucked anyway. How was *yours*?"

"I watched a bunch of movies: *Apocalypse Now, Platoon, The Deer Hunter, Full Metal Jacket* and *Coming Home*." Eddie, a Vietnam veteran, remained fascinated by that unpopular war and those Hollywood movies about it. Eddie became an opium and hashish dealer while in uniform and pressured many young Marines into submitting sexually to him.

"You're so nostalgic about 'Nam. Don't you know that that war was a black eye for America that we're still trying to cope to grips with?"

"Maybe." Eddie slapped the top of his desk. "But think of the fun *I* had!"

The Kits, in one of Vancouver's most fashionable districts, was a neighborhood cinema, a huge movie house, the kind of business that was disappearing forever. Rents were outrageously high and Andy wondered how long the Kits would keep running before some greedy developer would buy it, close it, demolish it and replace it with a twenty-story condo. For the time being, the theatre stayed open, and this was "Classics Week," and maybe two dozen people had shown up for *Roman Holiday*, some lame flick from a zillion years ago. Andy gave the washrooms a quick check and hurried over to the candy counter to visit with Anita Feist, the popcorn girl. The Kits sold organically grown, air-popped popcorn topped with real butter, not "golden topping," the nasty shit the huge theatre chains used. The Kits also sold fruit juice instead of sodas and home-baked cookies and brownies rather than candy bars. Andy and Anita both wore old-fashioned uniforms; she looked to him like a hospital candy-striper in hers.

"So, Andy," she said, "how was life in the psych ward? Meet lots of people interesting people?"

"Fuckin' boring." He handed her two dollars. "Give me a brownie."

She smiled. "Coming up." She reached down into the display case, pulled out a cellophane-wrapped brownie and handed it to him. "You don't seem like a psych-ward boy. You seem like a normal boy. A nice boy."

He unwrapped the brownie, stuck one end into his mouth and gestured for Anita to lean over towards him. She smiled as she did so, nibbling at the other end of the brownie until the snack became smaller and their mouths were an inch apart. As the brownie disappeared between them, their lips clung together in a long, moist kiss.

"Too yummy," she said, licking her lips. "You're a good kisser." Then, "Oh, fuck, here comes Eddie. Gotta look busy."

She started tidying up behind the counter while Andy started sweeping up imaginary popcorn spills. By then he needed to go to the front door to tear tickets for the second movie of the evening, *Bringing Up Baby*. The first people were old folks who got in free. Management had a longstanding policy: Senior citizens never pay nor have to stand in line. Many times Andy had seen popular movies attract a few hundred people to the Kits, the first of whom waited

45 minutes for the doors to open. Then, three minutes before management unlocked the box office, some old people would traipse up to the front of the line and get in without paying. How unfair was that to the paying customers at the front of the line? Andy asked himself.

By and by Eddie came up to him. "I'll relieve you. Go help clean up the auditorium."

Andy nodded and did as told. He looked up and saw a forty-foot still image of Cary Grant on the movie screen. At that moment Andy knew his life as he had known it was over. Cary Grant was a prince among men, a tall, towering example of what a man could and should be. He decided that Cary Grant was the man he would aspire to be. Andy had promised himself a hundred times or more than he would get his shit together and become a new sort of man, but that day had simply never arrived. Now a voice inside his head said, "School's out, mofo—time to make those changes and become that new man!" That huge image of Grant was the sign he had been waiting for. He knew he needed to grow up and become a man— and knew he could do it.

After work, he walked home, pondering his future. From here on out he would try his best at everything and, ideally, find something he could do very well. He wanted to learn something and find himself. No more laziness and sloughing off. Time to get his shit together and show the world the *real* Andy Rae.

He ate a bowl of granola just before bedtime and retired with his copy of William Styron's novel. By morning he had mentally written most of his book report as his mother emerged from her bedroom, yawning and stretching as she poured herself a cup of coffee. He had not yet taken his medication but that was O.K. He felt better than alive.

He told himself that doing homework during breakfast with a clear head was definitely better than starting the day up coming down from a drug binge. For a moment he feared that his mother would start ragging on him about staying up all night, but when she saw that he was doing schoolwork, she just smiled at him and said good morning. She fixed him a mediocre breakfast, and he assured her it was delicious as he devoured it as he checked the spelling on his school assignment.

Andy on his way to school thought of Cary Grant. The great man, the legendary American movie actor. If a kid like Andy wanted a hero, what better man to emulate? He told himself big changes were about to happen in the life of Andy Rae. He passed by a garbage can and tossed his Pall Malls into it, then his Bic lighter. No more smoking; no more Internet masturbation. That kind of shit was just a drain on his precious resources. It's all over, God! I'm yours now! Help me to grow up and become a man! He whistled a pretty tune as he walked. He had taken the long way to school so as to get in a little exercise and enjoy the morning. The air was redolent with the fresh smells of morning. He sniffed and smiled at the wonderful aromas. Life could be just too wonderful at times.

Just then he heard a sweet female voice and turned around. Babs, a pretty girl from one of his classes caught up with him and they walked together. He started saying hip, clever, funny things to her, things he had never said to anyone else. Things Cary Grant would say to an attractive female acquaintance.

Her hair and eyes were beautiful. She laughed hard at his rap, the way audiences roared at the Eddie Murphy and Richard Pryor concert movies he had seen on Netflix. The more he said, the more he busted her up. He bragged about how he would become the next Sean Penn, and when he wasn't starring in Oscar-winning movies, he would become a hockey great like Wayne Gretzky and win the Stanley Cup for his beloved Vancouver Canucks. Suddenly serious, she nodded at him, saying that *he*, of all the boys she knew, could go out into the cruel world and do those really big things.

He asked her to the school dance and she said yes. Her answer freaked him out because he didn't think he had a shot at a chick like her. She giggled, squeezed his hand and kissed his cheek.

"You better do something about that big zit on your face," said Babs.

Andy swallowed hard. He felt his race redden with humiliation and his limbs suddenly freeze. Yet he forced himself to walk along with her until she went faster and faster, as if to break free of him. He had to hurry up and soon grew winded. They rounded the corner and Andy spied Jessman and a half-dozen other school jocks. Tracie waved and smiled, and so did Andy, though he wasn't sure why, and he hoped Jessman might wave back. Instead, the big boy threw down his Dodgers cap and ran at him.

Petrified, Andy looked around and saw a large crowd beginning to form around him. Hardly an inexperienced fighter, he managed to get his wits together enough to step away from Jessman's roundhouse swing and punched him in the ear so hard that Jessman cried out. Andy assumed a boxing stance and fired as many punches as he could into Jessman's face, stunning but not hurting him. Andy split the kid's lip, then slammed his foot into Jessman's testicles. The bigger boy went down, and Andy, utterly exhausted, picked up a rock but lacked the energy to bash Jessman in the eye.

Jessman grinned as he struggled to his feet. "Nothin' left in the gas tank, eh, Rae?" The crowd roared as Jessman pounded Andy once, breaking his nose. Andy feared he would faint from the pain as Jessman fired a half-dozen more punches, severely bruising Andy's eyes and mouth. "Oh, goof! I can't believe how ugly I'm making you!"

"Stop it!" screamed Babs Charlton. "You're twice his size! You'll kill him!"

"Kiss my ass, bitch! How could you spend any time with him? He's such a fuckin' goof!" To Andy he said, "Do you know what a fuckin' *goof* you are?"

"He helped me with English," she said.

"Did *you* help *him* get his little cock hard?" Jessman retorted.

Andy just stood there, trying hard not to faint. His face hurt all over.

"If you ever bug me again, I'll kill you," Jessman said, kneeing Andy in the scrotum. Andy tried not to faint or vomit.

"Strip him!" someone called out. The crowd cheered.

"As you wish," Jessman said, bowing. He reached over and ripped off Andy's Levi's, then his underpants.

Andy, his face on fire and tears spilling out of his eyes, covered his penis and scrotum with his hands and charged past the laughing crowd. He could feel the wind on his bare ass as he raced home.

His mother had left for work, fortunately. He stripped and showered, crying loudly and passionately. He took a few of his old lady's Tylenol 3s and headed to the local arcade.

That night, stoned on codeine and malt liquor, Andy went to work. In the manager's office he told Eddie Bonzai all about that day's misadventure. He felt the need to confide in *someone*.

Andy went on and on about idolizing Cary Grant and how he was preoccupied with a certain beauty at school named Babs Charlton. "I've heard enough," said Eddie, holding up his hand to shush Andy. "That's all hormones talking. You'll care much less about that chick in a couple of weeks."

"I don't know what to do," said Andy, all hangdog.

"*I* do. Save your pennies and get a Mustang, a ragtop in midnight blue. That's what the chicks want—they don't give a *fuck* about the guy inside the car, they just want to ride around in the car and have the guy buy them all kinds of fun shit. You need to have attitude, not gratitude. Shit, man! Don't you know this already?"

Eddie seemed to have a real attitude himself that night. "Maybe you should get a factory job and keep your night job here. Are you hearing me, Andy? Or are you just totally stoned on goofballs? Anyway, your self-pity makes me want to laugh at you."

Then Eddie told him of a quick, easy way to make some money.

"You want me to give you a blow job?" asked Andy, incredulous. "For real?"

"Do I look like I'm bullshitting?" Eddie asked,

peeling a hundred-dollar bill off of a roll.

Andy, ready to vomit all that malt liquor he had guzzled, made a face and looked past Eddie for the longest time. But presently he knelt at Eddie's lap, staring at the manager's decent-sized, uncut cock.

Closing his eyes, Andy pretended he was a zillion miles away, watching himself as he accepted Eddie's half-boner into his mouth and began blowing his boss. He tried really, really hard not to think about what he was doing as he sucked harder and harder so the ordeal would be over with as soon as possible.

Eddie started holding Andy's head and guiding him up and down. "Weird, isn't it?" the man asked, chuckling at the paradox. "You're giving me a blow job so you can get some pussy. Life's a crazy thing."

Sighing, Eddie threw back his head and pumped his hips slowly as Andy kept at him.

The office was right next to the auditorium and Andy soon heard the unmistakable albeit muffled sound of Audrey Hepburn's voice as she played a scene with Cary Grant. Disgusted with himself, Andy tried to pull away, but Eddie forced his stiff penis father into Andy's mouth. "Pay no attention to Audrey Hepburn. She's old or dead by now. Her titties are all shriveled up."

Andy raised his head up anyway, as if Audrey Hepburn were there in the office, frowning at the boy for degrading himself. Eddie slapped his face and said, "Get busy. You took my money, now you're gonna eat my meat!"

Eddie grabbed Andy's head hard and with all his strength forced the boy's head up and down like a plumber using a plunger on a backed-up toilet. He talked dirty until his cock, insanely stiff, could stand no more and he ejaculated into Andy's mouth. As he pulled out his penis, he slapped the kid as hard as he could and yelled, "Not done yet. Swallow or you don't get the money." Andy, looking as docile as a Hindu cow, did as told.

ABOUT THE AUTHOR

George Onstot was born and raised in San Francisco but has lived near Vancouver for many years. He is still trying to decide what he wants to be when he grows up, whenever that happens.